GODDESS
of the
WILD THING

Paul DeBlassie III

HALLOWED REALMS
PRESS

GODDESS of THE WILD THING
Published by Hallowed Realms Press
Copyright © 2017 Paul DeBlassie III

Cover Design and Formatting by The Book Khaleesi
Editing by The Editing Hall

ISBN: 978-0-578-57885-9
Library of Congress Control Number: 2017910355

Printed in the United States of America

ALSO by PAUL DEBLASSIE III

Goddess of Everything

The Unholy

WHAT READERS ARE SAYING

"Paul DeBlassie III has an extraordinary ability to pull the reader into his mythical world, and the special effect depictions drawn within my mind while reading Goddess of the Wild Thing could easily match up with some of the most gruesome of horror stories on film. He transports you through an amazing spiritual journey exploring the power of fate and love. Packed with action, suspense and even romance, Dr. DeBlassie has written a truly brilliant and riveting supernatural story!"

- Tamara Ferguson
International, multi-award-winning author

"Paul DeBlassie III has a wicked gift in writing psychological thrillers, and he does it in a way I have never experienced before. In Goddess of the Wild Thing, he gave me a glimpse into his reflections, inviting me to draw closer to the dark side. His writing is rich with supernatural symbolism and, when all is resolved, deeply empowering."

- Uvi Poznansky
Artist and award-winning author

"Goddess of the Wild Thing is a psychic and erotic feminist manifesto! Twisted turns of love and fate take us on a literary adventure into a woman's fears and desires. Dr. DeBlassie conjures a paranormal thriller in which a woman's life depends on discovering whether bad love is better than no love. Goddess of the Wild Thing left me breathless and stunned."

~ Lorraine Carey
International, award-winning author

"Goddess of the Wild Thing by Paul DeBlassie III brilliantly couples his in-depth knowledge of the human mind and behavior with his love of lore, imaginatively knitting a deeply psychological and esoteric story that will keep you turning the page. I could picture clearly the fantastical sense of place… a must-read magical tale."

- Luna Saint Claire
Author of The Sleeping Serpent

"Dr. DeBlassie, author of the multiple-award-winning The Unholy, produced another novel with depth, action, and spirit in Goddess of the Wild Thing. For centuries we've struggled with whether bad love is better than no love. In this paranormal thriller, a fierce woman tackles the question with determination and fire."

~ Rayna Noire
Author of the Pagan Eyes Series

Dedication

~GWT

Mirrors, which scoop up the beauty that has streamed from their face and gather it back, into themselves, entire.

~ Rainer Maria Rilke
"The Second Elegy"

CHAPTER 1

Bad love is better than no love? Can't buy it. Don't want to buy it." Eve spoke in a clipped fashion as she walked hurriedly along the downtown street with her longtime friend, Shirley. Both women were of strong bearing and fierce countenance.

Eve was a single, auburn-haired, thirty-eight-year-old professor of esoteric studies at the University of Aztlan. Men, far and wide and from all walks of life, described her as a bronze-skinned, magical beauty, emotionally weathered but determined. Her life continuously hung in the balance, an unnerving play between love and an absence of love. For too long, she'd been alone, struggling against what seemed inevitable.

Shirley, a sharp-featured redhead, shook her head in disagreement but stayed silent. Sometimes Shirley and Eve got along. Sometimes they didn't. This was one of the "didn't" times. Didn't matter to Eve which way it went, just as long as they stayed trying to see things through.

Eve didn't try to break the tension. She let the fire burn. Best to let it be. The heat and the boil let things cook. After a bit, Eve took a sip of the mental broth and went on, "What I'm saying is women need love, and it's a tough thing, a wild thing. It's got good, and it's got bad. It's tough to find your way through."

They turned the corner, less than two blocks now from the old metaphysical bookstore, where they sought the counsel of one older and wiser in matters of the troubled and lonely heart.

Eve always kept an eye out along the edgy, nighttime streets of downtown Aztlan del Sur. Muggings, assaults, and the discharge of barrio gang Berettas and Glocks took the innocent and naïve sometimes by fatal surprise. Black asphalt was illuminated by sheens of autumn rains along with green, blue, and red neon lights casting an eerie glow.

Along the urban streetscape, Eve had encountered her fair share of nerve-fraying relationship thrills and chills. Many a knockdown, drag-out yelling match with men who turned out to be no more than one more of the same old thing.

She picked up her brisk walk, as did Shirley, a caring and seasoned physician of the same age who also sought answers to questions about life, love, and men. It was nothing medicine could answer, she and Eve had decided in many of their late-night conversations. Out of that sacred elixir-fueled ritual grew their sisterly conviction that only by living things out, and living them true, could light be cast on the dark corners of human need and human limits.

Shirley spoke up, "Maybe we just gotta give it up, and say there's no good out there and no damn good men." Shirley spat on the sidewalk, as she was prone to do when attitudes turned south and a pissed-off mood overrode a physician's reserve. A petite woman, hovering around five-foot-three, she was a spitfire to friends and foes. Her red hair was a fine match for her spicy temperament. She never hesitated to snap her tongue, making an envious woman or cocky man shrivel and long to crawl into a nearby hole and cry. Shirley lived as a healer and a warrior, a woman who cared tenderly for the hurting and raged viciously at pretense and abuse.

Eve, Shirley, and two other friends, Tanya and Samantha, were plagued by man troubles the way pollution settles in during dusty days and humid nights in the Middle Rio Grande Valley of Aztlan del Sur. They were four esteemed, professional women who could have any man they chose. Yet time and again, they went for the lower, the worse, the bad. They sabotaged the good, the permanent.

Commitment was a frightening consideration for four women who'd suffered childhoods of parental dysfunctional neglect and split-ups. They often quipped, "We found each other because like finds like."

Tonight, Eve's troubles were front and center. She'd done it again or at least worried she had. The glitch in the man was in the type she attracted: charmers—striking and untrue.

Suffering had begun. Time was critical. To stick it out or get out was her dilemma. Things with a new man had taken a terrifying turn.

Unending man dramas weren't necessary to life and well-being. She was educated, had plenty of common sense, and was street-smart. Countless members of the male species spoke of her in hushed tones at the cantina, in university hallways, and at social events when friends and colleagues were relaxed and enjoying themselves during the cool, high-desert nights. The thought of hooking up with the most desirable of fantasy felines for the evening rippled through the undercurrent of verbal exchange. She should be able to attract the right kind of man, one who was kind and caring and didn't bring tidal waves of emotional drama.

Eve had no time to waste. She needed the counsel of her trusted friend and spiritual guide. This turn of events was unlike any she'd ever encountered. It was violent and bloody and made her fear for her safety.

This new fellow had seemed genuine, courtly, romantic, and hot. He gave off a world-wise and street savvy vibe. There was a gentleness and sensitivity to him, more so than the typical single, middle-aged male on the lookout for female companionship and mind-blowing times.

However, she'd unwittingly found trouble and needed guidance from Graciéla, a seventy-eight-year-old wise woman, crone, and seer into confusing matters of the heart. Graciéla waited for Eve at the Sage Metaphysical Bookstore where she served as resident manager for an absentee owner. Even after an exhausting day of seeing one desperate soul after another, Graciéla agreed that Eve's situation was critical. She'd stay late for a friend and frightened soul.

Eve had to park blocks from the store because lately, downtown had become a hub of clubs, theaters, and trendy restaurants appealing to a congestion of new money and hot times. Close-in parking was locked up by happy hour, so blocks away was her only choice. She caught herself looking nervously from side to side and down twilight-shadowed alleyways as she hurried along the cracked sidewalk. She felt safer along these edgy streets with Shirley by her side, a genuine person and mystic cohort.

"Eve, honey…" Shirley paused before going on.

Eve knew Shirley hesitated because she was trying to be conciliatory—not an easy talent for a hard-bitten woman.

The pause passed. "On the other hand, maybe if bad love is what we get, bad love is *just* what we take. If there's something better, I'm in… just saying I've never seen it. Till I do, I for one gotta go with what I get." Her look toughened. "It's just not come my way, and I'm not holding a sure-to-turn-me-blue breath." A tough attitude toward life, love, and men was her stock-in-trade.

Eve smiled a bit. She loved her friend and all her rough spots and edges. There were people who were mean but not nasty, malicious, or toxic. Shirley was hardened and mean but only when and if she needed to be.

Shirley's hair floated a few inches away from her shoulders, static currents conjuring magic. Eve's peripheral vision caught the streaks of what she imagined as a bonfire during a war dance. Shirley spoke from experience, a woman smitten by man potential going south quicker than a rattler hisses and bites.

Eve kept up her pace as she contemplated Shirley's words. Settling for less than what she wanted was no good. It left her cold and empty. It was definitely no good. Plus, Shirley didn't know the whole story, only that gloom about the prospect of men and love had descended, and Eve was taking it hard.

"Bad love's a risk, Shirley. No good for me. If I need to cut this thing short, so be it. But I'd rather see it through. Maybe there's a chance that the bad I'm afraid of isn't there. Maybe I'm blowing it up into something it isn't. Maybe there's good and I'm thinking it's bad. So if the good is down deep, real deep—I want to hold on and give it a chance." Eve pondered the words as a light rain started up. Then she went on, "I need to hear what Graciéla has to say. I'd like to give things a chance. I'm not giving up unless there's no way out of emotional dead-ends and never-ending heartache."

Mists formed along the edges of the potholed asphalt and cracked sidewalks. They twisted and curled, arising out of a subterranean ether sphere. Usually, they arose during the early morning and hovered inches above the downtown park's green expanse, hardly ever at night with its fading daytime desert heat, and hardly ever along the paved spaces. Darkness descended and pressed down like a heavy hand, edgy and ominous.

Seasoned to the downtown streets, only a quick chill shot up Eve's spine as a rat ran alongside the gutter before disappearing down a rusted grate. Memories of days when the sight of a street rat by her feet made her scream and dash for the hood of the nearest vehicle brought a silent chuckle. Shirley hadn't said anything, so Eve went on, "When bad comes, it takes time to figure out what to do. Sometimes, there's more to it than meets the eye."

Shirley stayed quiet the way she did when she either disagreed or was simply thinking.

Eve couldn't tell which, even after years of heartfelt friendship. They spotted the bookstore a block away.

Shirley finally spoke up, "Just saying, Eve, that whatever is going on, nothing is worth having no love. I think I'd rather keep the thought of it, the fantasy, and let go of the rest. There is bad, but the fantasy, the ideal is there too. And the fantasy can stay and make up for the rest."

Eve stopped walking, looked at Shirley, and shook her head. "Bad love is no love, Shirley—no love at all." Her blood pressure rose, heat and tingling along her neck and ears. She needed to say more about Shirley's bullshit idea. She didn't want it stuck in her head. Whatever she didn't speak up about, stayed stuck and kept going round and round. Eve didn't like it one bit when she let that infernal fly keep up its mental buzzing.

She couldn't stop herself. "Goddammit, Shirley. There's more to love than illusion. I'll clear through the junk and find the real thing. If this thing is junk, I'm not going to ride it for the thrill. I need to trash what's trash. Fantasies are just that, fantasies. I want what's real. Doesn't have to be perfect—just real."

Eve was the softer of the two friends, but whenever Shirley got under her skin, she got fired up. She couldn't let wrong-mindedness and messed-up thinking pass, wouldn't compromise principle. Eve wouldn't stop herself from saying what she needed to say when she needed to say it, lest a twisted notion keep itself hidden and locked away in Shirley's mind, and then spring up like a jack-in-the-box nightmare, playing out a terrifying relational scenario because she didn't say no when she needed to.

She wished she'd been strong with men in a consistent fashion. But men were tough, their own kind of problem, and she was convinced that a woman seeing her way through relationships with them to any productive end was an art form. They messed with her mind, messed with feelings, messed with judgment, messed with a well-meaning and sincere woman.

She'd developed the habit of spitting like Shirley. In the gutter. She felt the urge. She spat. It was a quick way of getting what was inside, out. Shirley was a habit. And habits were addictive.

She walked on as butterflies lit through her stomach. The man she'd fallen for was Aztlan's most notorious criminal lawyer, Sam Shear, respected and feared. Eve's troubles had started with a threat. It set her on edge, same as a nudge while gazing down the Grand Canyon's North Rim.

Bird's blood painted a witch's warning: *Flee or Die ~ Man is Mine*. It was scrawled on the front lintel of her university-area, adobe home. She was torn between fear and anger over the cohort of doves—necks snapped and torsos crushed—scattered along her driveway.

Eve and Shirley turned the corner to the hundred-year-old red brick building that housed the Sage Metaphysical Bookstore. Eve opened the chipped, turquoise-colored pine door. An antique, tiny brass bell, affixed to the lintel, chimed. The door creaked closed.

Things felt strange, though. The store's lights were turned off. Strange. The smell of sulfur and smoke wafting through the way-too-still atmosphere. Strange. The utter silence of the hallowed realm. Strange.

Crystals dangling from sterling silver chains attached to display stands began to sway unevenly, unnervingly. Eve and Shirley looked around the eerily silent store. It was late in the day, but a few folks always hung around.

Soaking up the good vibrations right to the end, Graciéla often quipped.

Shirley whispered, "Hot damn, Eve. You sure it's okay we're here? It's like Graciéla wasn't expecting us. There's something bad here. I don't like it." Shirley never backed away from anything, but she hesitated before walking any farther into the old store.

The bell above the entrance jamb kept ringing, erratic and harsh. Eve turned and looked. It stopped. She continued to nervously scan the familiar space, quickly moving past the bookcases of mythic lore, magical history, and enigmatic rites.

Hours before at her home, beneath the witch's bloody words, mirror shards had been aligned on the concrete pavement, pointed edges outward. As Eve looked down at the warbled pieces, she saw her features, distorted, pained, and outraged. The memory flashed as bright as the midday sun along the white screen of Eve's mind.

Cautiously, she moved to the back kitchen where she and Graciéla usually talked over a pot of green tea. Many a day, Eve found consolation and insight in this sacred space. More times than she could recall, the two had shared tender feelings, confrontations, and tears.

From the threshold of the kitchen, she spotted the aged, tin-framed mirror on the far side of the room. It hung on the wall behind Graciéla's chair, askew with glass cracked and shattered. An ember at the center of the mirror's wooden backing glowed a fading red. Filaments of gray smoke curled downward, the stench of sulfur permeating the little room.

The back door was shut, deadbolt in place. She entered the tiny kitchen. Shirley was an uncertain step behind. Eve's breath caught. Graciéla lay slumped on the floor next to the scarred oak table, head twisted oddly to the side. Eve shakily approached. She bent down, instinct now more grounded and centered. Graciéla had taught her to focus her mind during a crisis. Panic was no match for a focused mind.

Shirley quickly went into physician emergency mode and checked Graciéla's carotid. She ordered, "Don't move her, Eve. We don't know for sure what happened. Need to call an ambulance. STAT!" She rose abruptly to her feet and tugged her phone out of her purse.

Eve knew one thing for sure; Graciéla's life force was gone. There was nothing Eve could do. She slumped back against the kitchen cabinets. Graciéla was dead. Evil had done its deed and covered its tracks.

Large shards of the mirror were scattered around Graciéla's head and neck. They had struck but not impaled flesh and bone, repelled by the wise woman's life force.

Eve closed her eyes, concentrated as Graciéla had taught, warmth turning to heat, rising from core to forehead. *Use your powers as I have taught you. Concentrate at the brow point. Learn not to hesitate. Do not doubt. Focus.* Graciéla's teachings would always be in her heart.

From her intuitive center, at the brow point, Eve witnessed the targeting of her friend. A witch committed violence on an image of Graciéla scrawled on a misty mirror. Eve's head jerked back with shock as she saw hatred unleashed through time and space. Tremors of fright and outrage shook through her core.

Gently, she opened her eyes, reoriented herself, and touched Graciéla's brow point, two fingers grazing the still-warm area. Closing her eyes again, she saw the distorted shape of a hateful woman, intuitively knowing it was the same person who'd threatened her and performed black magic against her closest friend.

Eve sharpened her focus. She saw the sharp nail of a witch's right finger tracing Graciéla's image on a foggy mirror in a grungy bathroom, touching the center of the mirror with a hatred so intense, the glass burned red hot. The mirror in Graciéla's kitchen cracked. Shards jettisoned at the old healer, then were magically warded off and drifted in place about her head and neck.

Graciéla's energy, tired as she was, had fended off the pointed shards. She hadn't been impaled. But the strain had ushered her from one world to the next. Death came not by the hand of another but by a weakened mind and body defending itself.

Eve, shaken, allowed her soft touch to stay on Graciéla's forehead, confirming the horror of what she'd seen. Shamanic wisdom, often discussed between the two kindred souls, spoke to Eve as she stroked her friend's head, remembering that death provided passage for one whose life had been well spent and whose time had come.

Eve wept.

After a few moments, she closed her friend's green eyes and whispered tenderly, "Always my friend, always love, always together in life and in death." She stood and wiped the tears from her eyes. A gray-brown, green-eyed, great horned owl hooted from the largest cottonwood branch outside the back window.

Eve heard Shirley finishing her call to the EMTs and police, and then walking to the front of the store to await their arrival.

One large shard lay at the end of the table, sharp tip pointed outward. It reflected Eve's image; a glowing red ember menacingly centered at the brow point.

New moon burial fires for Graciéla burned wild and high along the open terrain of Aztlan del Sur's West Mesa, perched nine miles from downtown, a plateau of endless desert and nighttime expanse. Eve and her three spiritual sisters encircled the bonfire and spread Graciéla's ashes into the lit cedar blaze. It sparked wildly and crackled fragrantly. Scents of the sacred wood cleansed the atmosphere.

The four and Graciéla were *mestizas* of Aztlan, the Southwestern United States' spiritual homeland for those of Mexican, Native, and distant European bloodlines. The old ones taught that the mystic dimension of Aztlan lingered outside of space and time. It was a high-desert region bordering the Rio Grande on which peoples for centuries had lived and died.

The four sisters who walked the path of life, nature, and the way of all things—as they had been taught by Graciéla— intoned their enchanted refrain:

She is lone and she is wild
She is Goddess of the Wild Thing
Her shout is as loud as thunder
Her breath as mighty winds
Her eyes flames of fire
She is moving
She is coming
She is near
She is Goddess
Goddess of the Wild Thing
She is moving
She is coming
She is near
You can't stop her
You can't stop her
Goddess of the Wild Thing
She is near
She is near

Lightning streaked the western horizon. Thunder clapped with resounding booms, shaking the sandstone plateau. Winds whipped up from the east, west, north, and south. They carried Graciéla's ashes skyward. Autumn night burst with star formations.

A gray-brown, green-eyed great horned owl hooted from atop a nearby basalt boulder inscribed with ancient petroglyphs. Meteoric lights exploded across the desert sky with hissing and whistling from the fire, taking the last of the healer's ashes onward.

CHAPTER 2

At home alone was no way for a rich man to spend his evenings, especially when the fires of desire burned brighter than the flames in the five-foot-high sandstone fireplace. Piñon logs playfully popped and cracked as he relaxed in his cavernous den. Newspapers hailed Sam Shear, Aztlan's infamous *abrogado*, as the most fearsome and expensive lawyer ever to set foot in the well-worn halls of Aztlan County criminal court. A six-foot-one, forty-three-year-old Caucasian with piercing, ice-blue eyes that tore to the bone, Sam Shear considered the legend that was Sam Shear.

He stretched out his heavily muscled, long arms and legs across the oxblood leather wraparound sofa. Gazing into the blaze steadied his mind from flights of fancy of nighttime encounters. Women were a bit of a hobby for Sam and were an altogether delightful way to loosen up and pass the time after engaging in life-and-death courtroom battles.

Memories of one woman in particular burned hot. Lingering gazes, touches, and conversation had been nothing short of mystifying. Talking to a woman for so long—hours—was unusual. Typically, he'd quickly get to the sensual issue at hand.

This woman, met in front of a metaphysical bookstore near his office and taken to dinner the next evening, stirred his emotions, passions, and locked his thoughts unlike any other female encounter in recent memory.

He'd never met a woman so striking, one whose effects lingered like the taste of a fine Argentinian malbec. His mouth watered as he remembered her. He couldn't forget the sense of her, her scent as fresh as wildflowers along the river, her laugh as soft and sincere as moonglow, her touch as soothing and arousing as exotic oils on dry skin.

After a sumptuously intense evening and night spent in his bed, he'd tried to contact her again, but there'd been no reply. His heart sank with each unreturned call. No one dared refuse his advances, the sustained interest of one so well known and powerful.

For now, he needed to move on from thoughts of this downtown enchantress and to what the evening had in store. There was more to life than one woman. Investing himself in one utterly delicious feline was not an interesting prospect. He played the field, stayed away from capture, and thereby prohibited what a woman could do to a vulnerable heart.

Fellow attorneys under his employ, pals one and all, were waiting for him downtown. He didn't want to be late. They always had a good night in store, typically of the sought-after Dionysian variety, intoxicating and revelrous. They'd meet up and walk from the office to their favorite downtown dive bar. Duties at the inner-city legal office completed, they looked forward to a night of lovely ladies and raucous times.

By late afternoon, Sam had won the release of Aztlan's

most notorious politico, a man whose criminal financial wheeling and dealing matched the viciousness of his marital life. Winning tough legal battles without so much as a tousled hair was common. Among other things, Sam was a lawyer of rhinoceros hide and a steel-trap mind.

Guiltier than dust was dry, the guy he'd freed had been brought up on racketeering and spousal abuse charges. Now, he'd see the light of day as a liberated man. Sam's two-hundred-and-fifty-thousand-dollar fee had been paid in advance. One down and over a hundred similar cases still awaited the tough-minded, some said mean-spirited rattlesnake-quick barrister.

After a day in the mouth of the judicial lion, Sam left his minions to finish the paperwork. He sped up the freeway in his black, custom-ordered, two hundred-thousand-dollar BMW 760 Li, exited on Tramway Road, and entered his sprawling twenty-acre, high-desert mountain estate.

It sat in the picturesque foothills of Aztlan del Sur, a setting that dazzled with mile-and-a-half-high desert sunlight flickering and twinkling on sand, stone, and glass like an exquisitely fashioned crystal. Mountains on either side of the sprawling hacienda were framed like pictures in the main room's clearstory windows. A crystalline-blue sky, and the late afternoon's well-stoked fire, roaring in the middle of a Venetian plaster den, cleared his mind of legal battling and maneuvering.

Entering the *Hacienda in the* Sky's twenty-foot, ironwood front doors, Sam had shed his ten-thousand-dollar Fioravanti 220-count precisely tailored suit. Shimmering cloth barely touched the limestone floor. Household staff silently lifted, ironed, and hung the garment in a cedar-lined closet of over forty similarly exorbitantly pricey ensembles.

After a half-hour swim in the black-tiled, Olympic-sized pool, followed by a refreshing sauna, Sam dressed. Linen pants and a banded shirt purchased on the island of Capri fit the occasion.

He sipped a meticulously prepared and shaken, dirty dry martini, transfixed by the piñon blaze in the perfectly tended hearth. It was evening, and Sam was hungry.

Eve and company sat at their local watering hole. *Los Muertos* Cantina was a downtown dive bar of renegade spirits, cheap booze, and fast and loose hustles. It gave lonely women a place to go, to see and be seen, despite the inevitable draw to just what they wanted to avoid.

Men, some needy and off-putting, others strategic and predatory, lined the dark cavern of ear-blasting music and ancient and scarred pine floorboards.

Eve frequently quipped that Los Muertos drew like a magnet. It was familiar and comforting, a place to go and blow off steam.

It was Friday Night Happy Hour, most often a time for kicking back, smart-ass jiving, and elixir-fueled emotional exorcisms. Tonight was different. They didn't give a whit about fun.

Craving release, exorcism of rage and grief, the four women savored the medicine of tried-and-true friendships and mind-clearing elixirs.

It was the evening after Graciéla's West Mesa memorial. They had decided to go ahead and meet for their sacred ceremony of strong drink and never-ending bonds. Theirs was a proclamation that good women kept going when the going got nasty and hope for love seemed gone for good.

Graciéla, a woman of passionate living and rowdy good times, would have approved.

The darkened bar mirror shimmered with images of four women woven together by strands of thick hair—blacks and browns, platinum blonde, and flaming red. They were the focus of attention for every empty-hearted, booze-laced male of the species that populated the dank downtown saloon.

The four pensive women went on sipping their respective drinks. They sat on their favorite torn-vinyl stools, torsos gently swaying with the bar's earthy music, a thumping mix of hard-edged blues and old-fashioned soul.

Uptight and relatively proper in their professions, the joint offered them respite. They let go of pretense and set into the mood of the place-dark, spontaneous, and edgy. They'd met here years back, started talking, and discovered common interests in the struggles of professional women, the mystery of magical rites such as yoga, and the unnerving and ongoing challenge of relating to men.

The cantina stood as their ceremonial place for asserting the tenacity of women wronged by raunchy men and, tonight, by a yet-unknown sorceress seasoned in the dark arts.

The tipsy four tapped their glasses as testament.

Eve, teary, said, "Graciéla was caught off guard. I know the police said there was no evidence of foul play. Dusting didn't reveal prints. No break-in."

"Shit," Shirley chimed in angrily as she sipped her whiskey and soda. "Day the sun turns red, I'll believe that. Someone badass threw a deadly curse. It was a turbo-charged psychic break-in, went right past the old one's spiritual immune system. This was more than old electrical wires in the wall sparking out and frightening Graciéla in her tired state."

She paused, wiped her fingers across her teary eyes, and swallowed hard, apparently fighting to keep her grief in check, then went on. "Graciéla was exhausted. That's for sure. I get it. Wires sparked, caught and burned through the wooden frame, going smack dab to the center of the mirror, and popped those shards out. She was startled, scared, then fell back. And that was that." She gritted her teeth before continuing, "But there was wickedness in it. I can feel it."

Eve added, "Well, Graciéla didn't believe in accidents. There were no coincidences. There's only synchronicity, a meeting of inner and outer events."

Shirley shook her head. "That's right, for sure. And I talked to neurologists at the autopsy. They said Graciéla suffered a stroke, an explosion of mirror neurons. It's rare, but happens more than we think. The brain overloads due to a weakening of the immune system. Blood vessels burst in a thousand directions. Her nervous system was overloaded."

The others listened intently. Eve was clearly consternated. "You hadn't told us. So, she died of a stroke. She was in *such* a weakened state?"

"I needed time," Shirley answered. "I had to do some research and make sense of it. Graciéla must have been terribly depleted. An explosion of mirror neurons occurs because of extreme exhaustion. Graciéla was seventy-eight and worn down by the cares and concerns for others."

Shirley wiped away the stream of tears she couldn't contain any longer. "At death, Graciéla hallucinated a mirror bursting into a dance of shards. The neurologist said victims see images flashing on all sides. An explosion of mirror neurons." She waited before going on, "Trouble was, of course, there's more to the story. A mirror actually burst. That lends eeriness to medical fact."

The others looked on, clearly shocked. They waited for more clarity. Eve offered, "It's synchronicity—a meeting of inner and outer realities."

They nodded as they stirred their drinks. Eve and company frequently spoke of synchronicity as operating behind the scenes of daily life. It exercised an uncanny influence with timing, events, and people.

Shirley, the tough-minded physician, continued, "Basically, mirror neurons help us with empathy. They mirror to us what people feel. They make us sensitive and compassionate. Graciéla—" Shirley swallowed hard, tears rolling down her cheeks then finished, "felt too much for too many."

Tanya and Samantha, the hustling, poised, and polished businesswomen of the sisterhood, looked at each other and arched their brows, eyes wide.

Tanya brushed her shoulder-length brown hair away from her face, catching the attention of an eager flush-faced male patron, which she ignored. Friends knew Tanya couldn't stand the thought of another quick romance loaded with nasty times and deadly impulses. She was a tough woman with a caring but often naïve heart.

She spoke up, "Graciéla was there for me when my spiritual light had gone out." Her voice quivered. "Graciéla always taught there was meaning behind tragedy." A far-off look spoke of tender times with a trusted spiritual mentor and friend.

Samantha, a platinum blonde, eye-catching feline, agreed with a nod and eyes full of tears. Graciéla had, for five years or more, taken care of Samantha when men led her down one street after another of empty promises and terrible heartache. "She was the mother I never had."

She hid her face in her hands and cried.

Eve felt for her friend, a woman who had been conned, manipulated, and burned by man after man, so unbearably that Eve knew Samantha had talked of wanting to die.

Samantha raised her head and wiped her eyes.

Graciéla had more than once kept her from the crazy edge of suicide, given comfort and wisdom to a soul who learned to pull herself back from crumbling edges.

After a few moments' silence, Tanya said, "A sage of Aztlan once wrote something like, 'What a warrior sees at her death is a personal matter. It could be anything—a bird, a light, or an unknown presence.'" She paused then added, "No telling what Graciéla saw in the explosion of images."

"Neuropsychologists say it has to do with the unconscious mind," Shirley added. "Unresolved issues are reflected back to us from a thousand directions. The mind brings things to closure."

Tanya grimaced. "Graciéla needed emotional closure before dying?"

"That's really no surprise," Eve said. "Graciéla definitely *was* human. Very human. It's how she knew all she knew, and how she could pass it on to younger women."

Eve felt a surge of sadness. Her friend was gone. No amount of tears would bring her back. She felt dry inside, empty and depleted from grief, and feared what lay ahead. However, the bar was no place to get lost in too much thinking or a flood of feeling. She got hold of herself and went on. "Graciéla told me, it's better to work things out early so later years can be easier. I think it was why she always went out of her way to help us. She said we were young enough to get things back on course, to learn from her, and what she'd gone through and knew to be true."

Eve remembered Graciéla confiding how a terrifying childhood of neglect and abuse within the *pueblo* had led her to discover the healing path.

Eve paused, swallowed, then shared again, "She told me there were things that would come together only at the end, when life finalizes our healing process. Then we naturally pass from this world to the next."

Eve sensed she should share more about Graciéla, a way to help friends who hadn't known as much about the wise woman of Aztlan del Sur. "Graciéla had a hard life on the reservation south of town. Tribal governance forced her to leave, thought she was a witch. Imagine that. From the scars of her past, she helped people heal, and the council banned her. They couldn't control her, so they sent her away."

No one spoke.

The four women had often talked about prejudice against the powers of a woman. Politics in tribes, states, and churches were dominated by men. When men felt threatened by a woman, they tried to stop her, the flow of energy, and the power. Graciéla called this power the Goddess.

On one of the last afternoons that Eve and Graciéla spoke, over a mug of green tea around the bookstore's kitchen table, she'd said, "Goddess stays hidden until she reveals herself in her own time. Each woman has her own path to Goddess. It's a challenging way, often filled with doubt. Intuition and dreams whisper their guidance." Graciéla spoke in a hushed and reverential tone about the Goddess. "Men stop the woman to stop the power. But you can't stop Goddess. She is coming. She is near." With the utterance of these words, Graciéla looked far and away as though into another dimension and repeated, "She is coming. She is near."

Eve continued with her friends. "They threw Graciéla out of the pueblo, but they couldn't stop her influence. She moved here, to Aztlan del Sur, and helped a lot of people. Without her, we'd be emotional and spiritual goners. She gave us guidance and hope."

She confided, "But I let her down. Her death after the threat was no coincidence. The shards at my home, the store, and Graciéla's demise. I shouldn't have asked her to stay. She was too tired, vulnerable."

"Eve, it does no damn good to blame yourself." Shirley placed a reassuring hand on her shoulder.

Eve took comfort from her friend, but memories of conversations with Graciéla pressed for attention. Graciéla had repeatedly instructed, "You're afraid to trust your instincts. They are natural—a natural magic." She'd often asserted, "Be a woman, or fear and disappear."

Eve knew what it meant to disappear. She was there one minute, and then gone. She doubted herself. Her mind left. Her body stayed. Her mind hovered in a far-off place, watching and waiting because the fear was too great. She alone had let the fear become what it was and now was alone with the spirit of Graciéla and her words. *Be a woman, or fear and disappear*.

Eve felt a surge of energy. She continued, "Graciéla taught that exhaustion lowers our psychic defenses. Bad things that are usually kept out, attack."

Graciéla had learned this from helping people heal. She remarked that dysfunctional people could become angry when kith and kin healed. Sick family wanted to keep sick family sick and became angry when someone changed or left. They sometimes tried to hurt Graciéla, but she warded them off, dreams warning her of intrusions or threats. "Sickness maintains the sick family balance. They want it because they know it, are familiar with it, and so it brings them comfort—deadly but familiar and comforting."

Eve continued, "She was always there for me, for us, and I didn't have her back." Eve, closing her eyes and cupping her hands over them, couldn't hold back her sorrow.

"If anything, *we* didn't have her back. I asked too much of her more than one time," said Samantha.

"Damn straight. So did I," echoed Tanya.

Eve wiped her eyes and caught her reflection in the bar's twenty-foot-long, reputedly haunted mirror. Her auburn mane tumbled and curled about her shoulders. The smoky-looking glass stretched ominously along the chipped and scarred century-old brick wall behind the bar. Despite her PhD in esoteric studies and standing as a tenured professor at the University of Aztlan, Eve never could shake the irrational feeling of threat and dread brought on by the bar mirror, an eeriness stronger with Graciéla's death.

An auspicious antique, many said it was a portal to an invisible world, a portal that swooped souls into another dimension. As smooth as a magical sleight of hand, the souls of these self-pitying creatures were ushered into the mirror's otherworldly realm. They'd be sitting on their red stools one minute, griping and stewing, and the next, they were gone like a puff of dust or murky dishwater down a drain.

They would disappear. Eve had never witnessed such a display, but local folk swore by it. She never contested the legend. The old glass sent shivers through her, and that was confirmation enough of something eerie and perhaps supernatural.

It was also said that the old looking glass read the soul,

and it wasn't ever wrong. Sometimes, the mirror would flicker violently, and sure as lightning through nighttime high-desert sky, the midpoint of the antique looking glass would pop out a shard into the right eye of its victim.

Word on the street said the mirror targeted liars, fools, and desperate souls. Some said there was a presence behind the mirror that shot the shard. It was a shadowy glimpse of a witch, they claimed, eyes saucer-wide. Liquor-plowed ravers honked on about a pointy black hat, a broom, a hissing cat with a curled tail, and a long, sharp, scary index fingernail. Witches, to the drunk and stupid, were no more than childish spook tales. To Eve and company, mestizas of the desert Southwest raised on tales of the paranormal, witches were as real as desert rattlers and three times as lethal.

A snarly, blubbery Caucasian man wobbled on the center stool. Sloppily dressed and sloshed, he cast a furtive, sidelong glance toward the four mestizas then snickered and muttered something about brown bitches.

Eve tried not to pay attention. The four knew the type. He was another corporate overnighter looking for what he could reel in.

His upper lip curled and drool edged out from the corners of his mouth. He leaned toward them, ready to make a move. His muttering continued, "Bagged one bitch next door, not too late to have more."

A crack ripped through the atmosphere, loud and harsh. Everyone cast a quick look outside as if thunder and lightning had just creased the night sky. The center of the mirror appeared as a drawn bow to the heavily liquored patrons, who pointed and gasped. Terror streaked across their faces. A couple reeled on their barstools. Another person fainted. Screams echoed throughout the dingy saloon.

The mirror careened inward then popped.

Shirley grabbed Eve's shoulder, tugging her away from the bar's edge. A whisk of Arctic-cold air breezed millimeters past Eve's left cheek. She brushed her cheek with her fingers and found traces of blood along the tips.

Teetering on the barstool, the portly gent yelled and cupped a palm to his right eyeball. Seconds later, he crashed to the red and black linoleum-tiled floor.

Liars, fools, and desperate souls.

CHAPTER 3

S weet Mary gazed outward from behind the antique barroom mirror. She was the incarnation of a woman of ancient repute: seductress, hag, and witch. Legends of Aztlan spoke of Michté, the Queen of Death, presider over the bones of the dead and soon-to-be dead.

As a young girl, Sweet Mary had been the Queen of Death's fervent devotee, praying nightly to a secretly stashed cardboard image. Then a haunting spirit, a monstrous specter, had appeared in the still of sleep and offered, "Soul for Michté." Little Mary, Sweet Mary, understood the meaning. Give everything, get everything.

Soul for Michté. Soul for Michté. Soul for Michté. The words had grown red hot, insistent, burned through the middle of her forehead. Their energy glistened and shot through her mind like electrical charges ripping through rubber encasements and setting everything in sight ablaze. *Soul for Michté. Soul for Michté. Soul for Michté.* Her mind blew into millions of pieces and every thought quivered with scorching energy that could target and destroy. The orphaned child—

used and abused by shadowy and cowled figures that slithered along the orphanage's corridors—with open arms and heart, received the dark stream of Michté into her veins.

Officials of the *Ecclesia Dei*, the powerful church of Aztlan, denounced Sweet Mary as the incarnation of the legendary Michté. "She was the daughter of darkness," they whispered to fellow clerics who confided to one another of their torment. She afflicted men who touched and took. They got the rash, the blisters, and the fevers that no medicine could cure. Yet they came, those who did not know of the curse but had heard of the budding beauty.

Sweet Mary was a bane.

In hushed tones within darkened church hallways, they spoke of her with reverence. She advanced the cause of the Ecclesia Dei throughout Aztlan because fear-drenched people craved their creed, the opiate of the desperate and needy.

Parishioners tossed hundreds of dollars into the offering plate so as to save themselves and their families from the likes of Sweet Mary and all manner of lurking evil. Sweet Mary was a big draw for the church, a regular topic for sermons. None, save one, had ever challenged the authority of the Ecclesia Dei.

The rival and challenger of the church and its then infamous archbishop was a young *curandera*, a medicine woman of northern Aztlan. The archbishop made his play, the curandera acted, and the outcome was the stuff of magic and legend, recorded in the fabled tale of *The Unholy*.

The four women mystics in the cantina were reputedly of the curandera's spiritual lineage. The professor, Eve, was the closest relation. They were women of natural magic and an unrelenting desire for life and love.

But they had yet to face their ultimate life challenge and

ultimate discovery. In the tradition of the medicine woman of Aztlan, the initiation into womanhood, into the mystic realm of a woman's natural magic happened through crisis. Love and the loss of love propelled the soul to journey into realms foreboding and forbidding.

Sweet Mary laughed as she thought of it, peril lurking, the winding and obscure path of women with an unrelenting desire for life and love. Sweet Mary knew better.

Sweet Mary's mother, the daughter of a wealthy rancher, had been a woman of natural magic until impregnated by the archbishop of historical infamy. Rather than face shunning by church members, she committed suicide during a self-induced abortion with a glass shard in a bathtub. Church people gossiped that months after the suicide, officials discovered a note in the woman's basement vault. It revealed the affair with the archbishop, the pregnancy, and the despair of a religiously tormented soul.

The fetus survived, some said by the devil's handiwork. Eerily it floated, eyes wide open, atop the cold bathtub water. Disowned by the family, priests secreted the child away to a renowned orphanage run by an Aztlan order of nuns, the Sisters of the Most Precious Innocents.

Before the arrival of the girl, the convent had prospered. After the girl's admittance, and especially once she reached pubescence, odd things, destructive events happened. Building after building underwent the ravages of spontaneous fires. Whole structures collapsed into piles of ashes and debris. Others stood blackened and badly damaged.

Of particular note was the fact that nuns suffered severe cuts. Shards of glass from windows, or more commonly, nearby mirrors broke off and flew at the necks and eyes of the consecrated virgins. They stopped short of the carotid and eyeball as though to act as a warning but not kill.

That may as well have ended the nuns. From that point on, they were like spiritual imbeciles. They performed prayers and rituals with soulless repetition, and their daily activities were weighed down with untreatable depression. The nunnery suffered a total depletion of funds, bankruptcy in the offing.

It spelled the demise of a once-vibrant convent of women dedicated to the Ecclesia Dei and its renowned Archbishop William Anarch. The young girl disappeared from the nunnery chock-full of nefarious vim, vigor, and vitality. Old nuns said the girl spiritually absorbed whatever she needed, however and whenever she needed it. She grabbed, did not stop grabbing, and the rest was psychic history.

"Bad seed," the superiors of the religious order said. It came through rancid psychological DNA, father to daughter. The plain-minded flock knew that the little girl was a chip off a hellacious block of bad religion that quashed life and love.

For Sweet Mary, as an eager adolescent, a mirror, black and lustrous, materialized in a dream. The Queen of Death, Michté, said, "Into the mirror gaze." She pointed at little Sweet Mary's brow point and screamed, *"Bagabi laca lama sabathani. Bagabi laca lama sabathani. Bagabi laca lama sabathani."* The little girl's brow point burned hot and burned red.

It was the first nightmare visitation after the pact. The Queen of Death's finger pressed so hard, little Sweet Mary's head and brain throbbed with terrible heat then burst into flames, before she awoke drenched in a sweat that soaked through sheets and mattress.

As an adult, Sweet Mary moved from the north to Aztlan del Sur. She needed to be away from the bastion of the Ecclesia Dei. Its hold in the south was not as strong. Aztlan del Sur bred unshriven souls ripe with cravings and lusts.

Sweet Mary ruled over the dead and soon-to-be dead of Aztlan del Sur. She *was* Michté. Dreaded up and down the Rio Grande, the Queen of Death raged within Sweet Mary. Tonight, the sinister force had descended to exquisitely lurid depths. She had done dastardly deeds. Evil, a tingling and glow of malice, lit through muscles, sinews, and veins.

Sweet Mary shivered.

Alerted to another woman encroaching on what was hers—the man she claimed as hers and hers alone—and further enraged by the rants of a foolish barroom man, she'd let loose a hellish might in furious displays of otherworldly powers.

It was a wicked gift.

Shards cracked loose, targeted, pierced, took down. Imperceptibly, the barroom mirror resealed, eye-blink quick. Other times, the mirrors remained cracked, a visible reminder, a warning.

Sweet Mary's dank apartment behind the mirror on the other side of the bar smelled of ruined lives, day-old urine soaked into sheets, and timeworn blood crusted along the tips of the forty-year-old gold shag carpet.

Aztlan folklore said Michté presided over matters of men and love gone bad. Bewitched corn gruel for an unfaithful husband or lover made for intestinal agony and death. A cast of the evil eye and a fire scar branded the adulterer on the left cheek. Enchanted liquor made the male member permanently wither, the man hanging himself from a lightning-charred cottonwood.

Sweet Mary relished mirrors.

She had a familial affinity for lethal shards. Images of vertical forearm slices and cuts to the carotid were easily imposed on the minds of vulnerable foes. Gashes to the uterine lining and tearing out a fetus in repose were another delight. Broken and pointed, the shards, when not left as a warning, were there one minute and gone the next.

In the bar, unholy cries and constant chaos lingered on in the dingy saloon. Everyone riveted frantic attention on the toppled, jowly drunk. He looked dead.

Earlier, Sweet Mary had sent him to the bar after she'd finished with him. Stunned—she always left men stunned—he zipped up and left the room, essence of soul sucked up and secreted away within the black heart of a man-ravenous witch. Sweet Mary ingested manhood like a glutton on pig fat.

When the portly gent bragged and scoffed, going in for his next target, Sweet Mary, from behind the opaque looking glass, observed and unleashed a pleasant, gratifying fury. The shard broke off and launched.

Men said what they said. Sweet Mary did what she did. They went down.

From the other side of the barroom mirror, Sweet Mary's pleasure deepened as terrified bar patrons, shifting from foot to foot, exchanged anxious blather. Nervous twitches, shaking and sobbing, and unconscious moaning afflicted men and women. Emotional fuses were blown.

A roomful of agitated gawkers, more than a handful reached for their phones to call 911. No one left the tortured bar atmosphere. A few stole glances into the gray-hued realm of the looking glass. Their gaze didn't linger long for fear of suffering the next shock, gash, and bloody ordeal. They didn't want to end up smeared along the sticky barroom floor.

She laughed and Michté, specter of innocent love spoiled and gone, howled and cried out from within Sweet Mary's breast.

Minutes after the ambulance left, a hush crept through the saloon like a slow sewage leak. A rat ran from the cantina's cramped bathroom and darted past the bar, its claws scratching across the heavily scarred plank floor. The place had turned quiet as a graveyard on a windless night.

Medical personnel reported the injured man suffered from an ocular hemorrhage. His eye vessels popped from acute hypertension caused by sudden fright. They couldn't detect signs of cuts from a discharged shard. The blood on his palm had actually oozed from a gash on his hand. The rim of steel along the barstool had a sharp edge.

Their explanation was that the man was drunk and panicked when he thought he saw his eye bloodied in the mirror, the horrid legend inflicted on another inebriated soul. He raked his palm along the stool's sharp edge then fell back and down.

Patrons insisted the mirror cracked and launched a shard into the loudmouthed fellow's retina. The shard struck and vanished, they insisted. Eve knew otherwise; the shard rested on the rusted steel bar top near the edge where she sat. No one noticed, and she wondered why they couldn't see what to her was readily apparent.

If the shard were a patron, it would have said something like, "See that! What are you going to do about it? I'm just a guy sitting here minding my own business." The mirror resealed.

Eve cleared her throat and noticed that there was no trace of blood on her fingertips. She shook her head, eyes wide and riveted on her three friends, all stunned by the quick turn of events. Her gaze returned to the sweep of the forty-foot-long bar.

The glass shard was gone.

CHAPTER 4

Near midnight, the four stepped into the nighttime drizzle of downtown Aztlan del Sur with its play of inner city, neon lights, nighttime catcalls, and sirens. The cantina never closed before two a.m., no matter the rowdiness or bloodshed, because one night was like another and patrons were used to and looked forward to the old bar with its spooky happenings.

Whoops and hollers from passing waxed and expertly chromed vintage lowriders signaled the start of weekend partying up and down Avenida del Oro. Glare hit the eyes hard. Screeching set the mind going in a million different directions, eyes scanning the scene.

The smudged glass door of the cantina closed behind the four tipsy women, muffling the blaring jukebox and sealing away the flashing neon blue, green, and red images of advertised beers, wines, and liquors offered in the tavern's darkened interior.

The four giggled drunkenly at their distorted reflections in the cantina's grimy, gritty windows. Sober thoughts, unbearable sadness, and shock from the evening had spilled into a liquor-laced oblivion. As always, they had stayed put at their barstools for the remainder of the evening and used the night's horror as an excuse to bend yet another elbow. The mood eventually turned lighter, playful, a relief from angst and grief.

Shirley's red hair, distorted and amplified in the window, blazed like a forest fire. The illusion flared out the tips of her hair across the smudged glass. It nipped at the chins and cheeks of the four, setting each head ablaze. They let out a quick gasp and stepped back a foot or two, shook their heads, and returned their eyes to the smeared glass.

Shirley's hair burned wildly. Samantha and Tanya's features turned harsh, cruel. Eve's face glowed with otherworldly luminescence. Her shoulder-length auburn hair exaggerated an already sculpted figure, a sudden and unsettling likeness to the Goddess of Aztlan, Tonatzé, the deity of feminine instinct, nature wild and free, love vital and constant.

The others pointed at Eve's image then moved their hands to their mouths. Eve was also taken aback. She'd never seen herself in such a state, forceful and sure, her eyes a piercing amber.

"Well, I'd say we exorcised the week's tension demons," Eve quipped. The others stayed silent and looked at her as if she were some strange presence. Eve stepped back from the window.

"Let's get a move on before things get any more bizarre." Samantha, words slurred and legs wobbly, said it and apparently meant it. "Hard liquor keeps hard-living women keeping on. Let's get ourselves out of here."

It was time to get home. They gave each other hugs,

raindrops mixing with their tears. Emotional reprieve returned as autumn rains through parched desert *arroyos*.

Eve staggered and drew a deep breath. She raised a pointed index finger to the sky, and in her most professorial voice proclaimed with a slur, "Hark! We call upon Gabriél, archangel of protection, to send us… cabs." Eve stumbled off the curb.

That did it. It broke the spell. The four roared with laughter. They bent over with tears streaming down their cheeks. Booze-intensified emotions lit through minds and jumped like sparks from unprotected copper cables.

Nighttime drizzle had ceased.

Wisps of humidity appeared to rise out of an ethersphere, forming into thin mists that obscured their feet. They pointed and feigned fright. "A little spooky. Mists are the memories of the gods." Eve's words widened their eyes.

She and the others, following her lead, bent down and played with the thin vapors.

Shirley stood upright and flicked the tips of her hair, strands prancing a devilish red and yellow under the direct cast of twenty-foot-tall wooden light poles. A loud crack with the jab of an electrical current raced through the atmosphere. Hearts quickened; breaths clutched. The four looked at the window, thinking it had shattered but it hadn't, and they broke loose with yet more laughter.

"Watch out flicking that red hair, Shirley," Tanya joked.

Laughter, contagious and rowdy, started up again, this time even more uncontrollable.

Samantha wobbled, causing lightheartedness and laughter to shift to crying. Normally, when not her soft and tender self, she tried to be stoic. She rarely cried, save for elixir-inspired moments.

"Oh shit! Shit! Shit! Shit! It's the Jameson blues. I shouldn't have had the fourth!" Samantha never could stop the stream of Jameson tears once they kicked in. Nothing ever worked and the way she was now, stomping her feet on the pavement, wouldn't work either. Yet, she kept it up and stomped her bronze-toned legs, calves firm from years of flamenco dancing. Finally, she ceased her angry movements, shoulders slumped, hands hanging by her side. "I can't believe Graciéla's dead. She was an old woman, but I thought she'd live forever. Now she's gone." Samantha hung her head low, seeming inconsolable.

Eve felt waves of grief for Samantha, knowing of her strong tie to Graciéla, a confidant and guide during the worst of times.

Three weeks before, Samantha had emerged from the downtown police station off Broadway and Lomas, her ex-boyfriend charged with stalking. She'd suffered from his antics for months before the police could do anything. Finally, he'd been caught peeping in her bedroom window around midnight after a female neighbor spotted him and called 911.

Minutes later, a police officer, who had been patrolling nearby, caught the fellow in the act. Samantha identified him as the one whom she'd already filed reports on. He'd been stalking her. He was another realtor who'd had a thing for her. She thought she'd brushed him off.

At first, it had been hard for her to understand the gent. Smooth talk and a charming manner lulled to sleep her usual cut-and-dried common sense. Her three friends had told Samantha the guy was too skilled.

They told her, "No one is that smooth. You want someone who lets their wrinkles show, or there's going to be trouble."

It had been hard for her soft soul to believe the worst

when she wanted to see the best.

So, there was trouble. Plenty of it. The fellow had a temper, bloodshot eyes nearly popping out of their sockets when he was pissed. Demands, threats, and peeping, not to mention the dozen red roses delivered with blooms snapped off, put an end to a freaky liaison of the most insane variety.

Graciéla had seen Samantha through, as she had each of the four—ordeals of life and love witnessed, cleansed, and helped to heal.

Now Samantha was going down, and Eve knew what she was like when she crashed and hit hard. Her terrible times were more than Jameson blues. Samantha's rocky emotions were the worst and roughest of any moods she'd ever seen, waves of black humor engulfing composure and sanity.

The three blamed Samantha's bad luck with the opposite sex on attention-grabbing good looks and a generous bosom. The wrong kind of guys lit on the bling, sparkle, and curves of such a sexy female, and dive bar types yielded nothing but trouble.

As if on cue, the women looked down the street. They saw four loud and robust men swaggering along from the end of the block. They were trouble, intent clear as their cocky walk.

They spotted Eve and company and froze, hungry male eyes riveted on the ladies.

Samantha's tears began to dry. She wiped them with the backs of her hands. She was unsteady, caught between passing grief and man distraction. She shook her head and furrowed her brow.

Men were a disturbance, and when that disturbance set in, it was hard to unhook. She looked at her friends like a deer caught in headlights. Then she nestled in close. They were motionless. The night shifted to still.

Yellowish fifty-year-old streetlights on their stooped wooden and splintered poles cast a surreal light over an ethereal scene. Smoldering male energy snaked down the path. The men exuded musky good looks. They were deadly as street drugs cooked and mainlined.

Bubbling, burning, aggressive.

Four professional men, three in tailored suits and one in fine linen, sporting expensive haircuts, took their hands out of their pockets and moved in. Their eyes were riveted. Distractions had been wiped away. Four women standing down the dimly lit street were the uncontestable point and destination.

Eve noticed they didn't blink. The front-runner, his blue-eyed gaze—she knew him. Her heart quickened, raced, and her mouth went dry as her head swam with a million thoughts. A stream of heat set loose inside her.

Their steps stayed sure and strong. These guys didn't know the meaning of being refused. Eve read faces the way she scanned street signs and lights: Go ahead, slow down, stop. These four dogged and mesmerizing faces were any woman's thrill and chill. Caution lit through the air. Gents who knew what they wanted and expected to get it were a snakebite, toxic if not lethal. She shook it off.

They were halfway down the short block, hadn't turned a head or uttered a word. Unspoken communication, instinctual drives drew the four to the felines. Eve couldn't move. She hated man paralysis. Such immobility lasted forever and longer. Her friends were also caught tight in the man vise. Moments lingered and sped by. A tilt-a-whirl late at night with a stomach full of junk food would've kicked out less nausea. She couldn't even move to spit. Bile crept up her throat and stayed there, stuck.

The men, three storefronts away, remained cocksure, set on the smoldering goods of the Aztlan del Sur street scene where four hot and fine women on a dark and humid night stood in place as though on command.

Memories of love gone bad with downtown bar types had been ditched with a quick grab, throttle, and toss. Experts were they in the finely honed art of emotional sleight of hand. They worked the mental trick and, for that instant, relished the trickery.

Bile ceased.

Fired-up hormones sent love history flying out of memory banks like bats rocketing out of an otherworldly cave. Eve's sense sharpened, neon lights preternaturally bright. Skin prickled with erotic eagerness. She felt euphoric, alive, and lusty. Oncoming man heat was a bottle of whiskey at the end of a soul-scorching day. Tongues sensuously rolled over lips.

The men approached.

"Ladies… good evening."

Women poured, sipped.

It burned.

Seconds stretched out.

The four women gazed transfixed at the silent and wide-eyed four men. They looked delicious. They looked innocent. They were, and they were not, eyes lined with experience and knowing.

Shimmering oasis water was everything to parched souls.

Front-runner fellow, the spokesman, wore an off-white,

linen shirt and pants that set him back an easy ten Ben Franklins. His eyes were on Eve. No one else apparently existed to him. His voice was rich. It was sensual. Its allure was a sip of exotic blends of Aztlan red wines. Blue eyes transfixed on brown. It was as if she alone mattered, was the matrix of his yearning and fantasy.

She knew him; they'd gone out. The night had been a fleshy and sweaty climax after climax in a grandiose, mountainside hacienda on a sumptuous and oversized goose down bed. Lips and tenderness quickened to passion, conjuring an utterly memorable and stunning erotic encounter.

Dark-haired, exquisitely tall, robust build, his eyes were clear as high-desert moonlight on a cloudless night. Confident, totally void of self-doubt or ill regard, he was the type of man who made women melt and beg the gods for just one night of undivided tending. And they were together, once more. He'd called her days ago, repeatedly, but she hadn't returned the call. Grief over Graciéla had taken up everything.

Adrenaline-laced attraction lit through Eve. Tautness gripped her gut. Magnetism was as palpable as sweet breezes after rain. Her knees were weak and her mind spun. *But pull back. Back. Don't go forward.*

Bad had happened and had to do with this man. The logic of it escaped her. She couldn't even pull his name to mind, so caught was she by the sight of him. She had to remember his name, struggled to as she gazed at his smoldering bearing.

Memory would sharpen because they'd done more than screwed. They had talked for hours, dipped into each other's lives and minds. It made him different, better and hotter. She'd fallen hard, the tug and pull of it afflicted every muscle, sinew, and joint.

Intensity, sexual heat, and magic made Eve's mind leave. She'd enter into a trance, psychologists said. It happened because of a woman's scars, trauma. But it wasn't all bad.

She craved it, extreme heat, burning intensity, trance. Addictive. Alive. Then she'd forget their names. That's why she needed to talk to Graciéla. Her fear of repeating old mistakes with bad men borne of witchy women was a constant threat.

One time, Eve and Graciéla, sipping their afternoon tea in the quiet of the kitchen, the old one confided, "Witches destroy love. When you love a man, there will be a witch. There will always be a witch in matters of love and men. You must find your power or lose your love and perhaps your life." Witches did what they did often without leaving a trace. But Eve knew evil. It threatened, aimed then struck.

Her mind hovered and looked on from above. Sexual chemistry wafted through the downtown nighttime atmosphere. Men and women kidded with one another, flirted, but eyes were on Eve and the striking fellow of imposing build and mesmerizing blue eyes. Sam. That was his name.

Sam Shear, infamous criminal lawyer and black magic mage of downtown Aztlan del Sur.

They stood, fixed in place on the downtown sidewalk outside the cantina. Eve couldn't have broken free of his charm if she'd wanted to. She didn't want to. Locked in place with a promising man, wonderment and tease in the heated mix, was not a bad place to be.

The inner voice started up again, and Eve quashed the visitation. Conscience could be such a nuisance. It doubled up on her, memories of love gone bad and day after day of unrelenting heartache. *Pull back. Back. Don't go forward.*

Eve petted it, soothed it down. Easing then smoothing, she quashed the sense of relational right and wrong. She flicked away the risk and danger like a psychic magician, turned a red flag into a throwaway Kleenex.

She took a deep breath. Man, handsome man, chiseled man, wore no cologne. She remembered the fresh and clean then salt and sweaty, the smell and taste of the man with no cologne. Eve hated cheap cologne; she preferred no cologne. Body memories strengthened, delightful and unbidden smell and taste sensations.

That night in bed was a time of flesh, sweat, and scents. He absorbed her contours, every inch of her ravished, crevices tingling then exploding. Tranced out and satisfied was a thing to behold for one observing from above.

It was the first time she'd felt so much so close. Her mind hovered but closer to her body than in previous encounters. A child's past can haunt her forever. A body never forgets what's gone bad even in the midst of good.

Lighthearted banter among the others kicked up. It blared, uncaring if passing walkers and gawking drivers heard. Hearts were atwitter. Men strutted, women sported coy glances and shy smiles. Mists rolled up from cracks in the sidewalk and curled lithely.

The gents and ladies carried on, swept into come-hither antics. Shoulders touched with playful finger grazes barely missing forbidden areas. The sexual electricity was so hot, red and blue sparks practically flew person to person.

Graciéla's image flickered along the white screen of Eve's mind, dizziness setting in. She couldn't help but sway from the force of the vision. She steadied her legs and stopped the hopefully imperceptible movement. Her old friend had a message, the power of the moment made it too hard to hear.

Eve tried to dismiss the image, but not her feelings for her friend. Still, Graciéla's presence remained palpable. Tears welled before Eve swallowed hard and gritted her teeth. Hollowness opened wide.

She shifted her attention to her friends. He did the same. They joked loud then louder, the group starry-eyed and loose. She pictured herself tumbling into a familiar abyss of infatuation and denial. Her stomach clenched. One-night stands were hit-the-spot hot but left a woman cold.

Freud called it repetition compulsion. It revisited bad love time and again because it was the only love they knew. Psychologists had told Eve of her bad love habit, one in which her friends also indulged. It was a drug. *The* drug. A street drug. Available. Addictive. Smooth and fine.

The inner voice called out once more, a song message, beseeching. It cried out, *Wish you would step back from that ledge, my friend*. Bad love never seemed bad.

Eve hushed the voice, but it wouldn't stop; she got pissed and gagged it. Sadness, grief, caution, and pain snapped loose, fell away, gone. Love was a drug. Smooth and fine. Addictive.

This time, things would be better. Smooth and fine and addictive.

Eve stepped closer to Sam.

His smile struck her as moon glow set against steely, blue eyes, cold and unnerving. A shudder shot through her. Maybe she shouldn't have gotten rid of her conscience, its voice persistent for a reason. Now, it'd been vanquished. It was best that she moved forward without trepidation.

"You are beautiful." Without reserve, he swept thick fingers through her long, wavy hair. Auburn strands and the luxurious heft of long curls that swept past her shoulders seemed to transfix him.

She recoiled. It was an intrusion. Violating. Entitled. All sorts of descriptors crowded her head to include *asshole*. Despite the past, she suddenly didn't like the guy. She was repulsed.

She pulled farther back. Unmasking took time, happened in varied ways, the unexpected, the truest. Entitled men were legions for a dime. Given their night together, maybe she shouldn't feel put off, revolted. But she did. And the instinct—revulsion—clung tightly. Her skin crawled, upper lip curling.

"Whoa… sorry, little lady. Didn't mean any offense." Patronizing tone and manner, hands raised in arrest, furthered the disgust. He hadn't come close to arrogance when they'd been alone. With other men, the *macho* uncoiled.

He flashed an ear-to-ear smile. His right eye twitched. He grazed his fingertips across the spot.

The twitch continued. Eve didn't divert her eyes. He'd been seen and couldn't hide. She didn't like a man who needed to hide. He wasn't the gentleman she'd been with the other night.

Eve cleared her head and moved closer, mestiza-brown eyes boring into Anglo steely blue. "No offense, huh?" She didn't know *this* macho guy, didn't want to. She dangled her manicured, red-painted nails before his unflinching gaze. Quick as a rattler, she mussed his gelled hair and wiped her hand on his fine linen threads. There'd been no gel four nights before. Gel guys were like greasy chicken and Chiclets, bad for your health and cheap. Ear-to-ear, she smiled. "No offense intended."

Frozen in place, the others had grown silent and watched. The atmosphere drew tight and brittle. Then one of the other guys broke into easy, contagious laughter. He tried to make as if Eve had been joking and that they'd finally caught on. A joke at a car wreck would've been catchier. Yet, Eve's friends went along with the jest, letting the forced humor spread and trying to ease up an uneasy situation, all the while eyeing her nervously.

Setting men straight wasn't new for Eve. As a professor, she lectured on feminist psychology. A reputation for sharp wit, a quick tongue, and intolerance for male peacocks followed her. Academic corridors were noted for their fair share of scholarly predators. She'd had none of it.

Toying with a woman wasn't tolerable to one who'd suffered at the hands of many a guy, who up front looked good but later revealed pitiful moves and sordid motives. Or, in Sam's case, they showed one side of themselves here and another there. They never were true, never could be counted on. Problems aplenty came from men who set the all-I-need-is-love stage for needy playthings.

Eve wasn't interested.

Graciéla said Eve had it in her to be strong and stay strong. Sometimes, Eve felt it but mainly she didn't. *You disappear. It's the easy way out.* Graciéla appeared beside her, materialized in her mind's eye. It was both comforting and distressing.

Sam looked nonplussed. Once he managed to flick away the twitch, he hadn't shown a thread of irritation. His face was wiped clean, clear, and flawless.

"Let's start over." He looked genuine as could be. "My name is Sam." He stretched out his hand, blue eyes caressing brown, his hair remaining as she'd fashioned it. He wanted to start afresh but also leave his mark on her. He didn't blink, eyes quiet and inviting, captivating. Scary.

Red lights flashed on the white screen of Eve's mind. He'd caught her off guard. Sam pulled it back together quick and now didn't flinch at her smart, gutsy and purposefully off-putting ways. This guy needed to be ended.

She didn't shake his hand. Graciéla looked back at her. She had walked down the street. Her image flickered then faded as she turned and walked on. She'd brought a firm presence, and Eve knew the strength from it would leave because strength always seemed to leave her. For the moment, she savored it.

He withdrew his hand then turned his lip up a bit and arched an eyebrow. Surprised but not offended, he offered, "I'm sorry. I was out of place." He bowed his head with an air of nobility. Practiced genuineness was a smooth devil.

Eve's temper rose. Her ears tingled with outrage, neck muscles straining. She caught herself squeezing her hands tight.

Sam's eyes locked on the rhythm of her hands. Then he looked back up at her, warmth creasing his hardened features.

"Ah… Eve, give the guy a chance. Let's have some fun," Samantha whispered in her left ear, leaning close to where Graciéla had been. The voice of a trusted friend mixed with potent liquor, endangering her resolve.

Samantha didn't go back and forth with men; she went with men, got what she wanted, moved on. Eve wavered, thought of their night together and the understanding look he was now giving her. *Samantha is a trusted friend, and fun is not a bad thing to have,* she told herself.

Sam offered his arm.

Images of Graciéla and her firm presence and words crossed her mind. *Go back on your feelings—fear and you disappear. It's the easy way out.* Each man, every time, brought fright, fear that there'd never be another guy, another time, another chance for love. For an instant, Eve thought she caught sight of Graciéla at the end of the block. Perhaps she had reappeared to help with the inevitable wavering.

"Yeah… Eve, come on, give the guy a chance," the other two chimed in. Three friends, who'd been together for a decade, didn't mean wrong but could be mistaken if under the influence of their favorite painkiller.

The other men waited, watched.

Eve gave a quick look down the block, squinted imperceptibly. There was no one there. The street lamp at the end of the *avenida* went out. Strength was a flitting thing. This time, things would be better. Eve disappeared. She took the offered arm, mind sober and empty.

CHAPTER 5

Inside the blaring cantina, everyone paired up, looking as if they'd been together for many memorable nights. Eve sat next to Sam at the rounded, red vinyl booth, a snug fit for eight cozy pals. She felt like a wind-whipped kite tethered to a fraying silk thread. Torn vinyl stuffing spilled out from seat indentations and the edges of the old booths.

The exit sign dimly pulsed over the steel back door, dents and scrapes from out-of-control bar brawls decorating the sturdy barrier. No one paid attention to the *nicho* sculpture set a few feet above the booth. It was the Goddess Tonatzé, Goddess of love and war. Her sacred refrain intoned within Eve's mind:

> *She is Goddess.*
> *She is Wild Thing.*
> *She is Goddess.*
> *She is Near.*

Aztlan legend held that the Goddess appeared at times of

need, readiness for discovery, her apparition heralded by the chant.

The polished black stone sculpture shone with refracted multicolored bar light, darkly radiant spears making the eyes squint. Flickering red votive candles illuminated the deity. Eve's breath caught in a moment of silent devotion. Her heart quickened.

Graciéla drew near. *Goddess whispers during waking hours, consolation and inspiration during times of need. A vision of the night, during sleep and dreams, brings guidance. Finally, at the time of discovery, she appears and speaks. The words change and the sound becomes eternal.*

She felt close as Eve's subtle breaths. *The old saying holds, hitting bottom means there's nowhere to look but up. Then Goddess comes. And the chant becomes eternal.* Graciéla was kind with her words, compassionate with her unfailing, invisible, presence.

Eve looked up at the Goddess.

Sam noticed her upward gaze. "Why look up there? I'm here, over here." He touched her chin and pointed to his smiling face. Macho was here to stay. Her stomach twisted and curled. Remaining with a narcissist was like looking for comfort by shooting up rat poison.

The edge of Sam's torn vinyl seat suddenly folded and sent him sliding to the scummy floor. He jerked his head up and reached for Eve's hand. A flash of a little boy, alone and lost, scampered across his face.

Eve watched him fall, looked down, smiled, and rose from her seat, stepping over him to leave.

A couple of sharp pops turned heads to the cantina's window. Flashes from handmade street weapons lit across downtown shadows. The bordering *barrio* was of the warring kind.

Halfway out the cantina, Eve stopped, her heart tightening. The barrio was a mestizo gangland. Natives had sunk to below a subsistent standard of living. Edginess on the streets made many a lad do impulsive things. More shots rang out.

Shooters were heard laughing and howling down the street, jacked up on Jack and white powder. Cops could no more spot and catch them than a tank could target a rat. They slipped into alleys with the guardianship of a quick sign of the cross and touch of fingertips to the lips.

The gunfire outside ceased. Half a minute crawled by, everyone quiet, on edge. Tension curled through the skanky cantina like wafts of smoke in a witch's lair. Sam had followed her. He put his arm around her. He gave her a squeeze.

His squeeze was a steel vise.

Time passed, drinks were downed, and the flirting heated up. Eve, her mind liquor-relaxed, had cautiously lowered her guard. She fantasized about the man beneath the clothes, couldn't help herself. Vodka on ice with a twist shifted vibes into realms both relaxed and erotic.

Her skin tingled, shivers racing up her arms and legs. A half hour ago might as well have been a lifetime. She scarcely recalled why she got up from her seat to leave. It was something about Sam's attitude; but that had gone, and with it, the man she'd known a few nights back had returned.

Sam's sexual energy was as palpable as his warm touch

along her shoulders. Currents of electricity shot up and down her spine and into the places unseen and intimate. He knew he pleased her and smiled with a nod.

Her fingers teased up and down the sleeves of his costly Italian sport coat. She fingered, caressed, goose bumps rippling along his neck beneath a sheen of perspiration. She knew he wasn't the only one who did the pleasing.

She held the picture of Sam in her head. The white-hot center of her mind held the man immobile. Bewitchment. Sam stayed fixated, snared.

She shouldn't do this but couldn't stop. Magic for personal gain never ended well. *Things should play out in their own way, not as human will concocts.* Graciéla's image flickered then faded. The old one wouldn't give up on a woman who'd often given up on herself. Eve smiled slightly. She was a woman whose powers could burn bright, and then go dark.

Her upper lip curled wickedly. It was an automatic movement. She didn't try to stop it. Adrenaline gave a nice buzz. Sam jerked back as though having touched a live electrical wire. Sparks flitted up and down the linen sleeve of his sport coat where Eve's finger had caressed it. Wisps of smoke floated thinly in the bar's shadowy stratosphere then vanished.

He hadn't noticed the ascending gray spirals when he caught sight of the smoldering little hole left in his jacket. "What the heck? Moths must have got into this. Or, just maybe, somebody has been up to naughtiness." He winked.

Eve lightly grazed the tiny area with her fingertips. "It's hot. Touch it." She raised her right eyebrow and smiled coyly.

Sam rolled his tongue over his lips, held Eve's gaze, and brushed the smoldering spot with the back of his hand. Then, with an arch of the brow, stated, "All gone." The hole was no more, the linen now one piece.

Eve had seen sparks trailing the movement of his hand. Static or magic, she couldn't guess. Her skin crawled. He grinned roguishly. The jukebox blared a tune about a magic, seductive woman. Sharply edged flames from red votive candles rose. Three inches above glass containers, they danced erratically. After another few sips of her drink, Eve's shock turned to intrigue.

Touching, kisses on cheeks, under-the-table caresses flitted back and forth between the sexes. Enjoyment ran delicious and plentiful as tapped microbrews and uncorked bottles of Aztlan's finest wines.

Languidly, Sam leaned back, widened his blue eyes as though sensing her thoughts. He smacked his hands together so loudly, patrons looked. Talking ceased. The final pulse and beat of a thumping song punctuated the silence.

Lightning ripped across the sky, windows rattling. Thunder reverberated across the old wooden panes. A warbling to the smeared glass cast an illusion of a platinum-haired witch. She pointed a sharpened nail at Eve and cackled. Eve turned to Sam, wondering if he'd seen the vile woman. She didn't ask. She quashed her shock. She pushed the image away from her mind. It was gone, and only Sam was there.

His blue eyes glinted like a trickster. A sinister gaze peered out from the cold, blue orbs, and then the wicked personality withdrew. Sam chuckled, table silent, dumbfounded. He winked at Eve, her lure taken, snapped.

It was hard to breathe. Eve gasped, felt dizzy, spread her elbows out to the side, and leaned back from the table. The cantina closed in and swirled; nausea dipped to the pit of her stomach.

A woman needs love, and it's a tough thing, a Wild Thing. It's got good, and it's got bad. And it's tough to find your way through. She'd said it to herself during times of confusion and disorientation, words reorienting and guiding.

Unbidden images of a well-trained warlock spun through her mind. They were known of in Aztlan, but she had never encountered one, the best of them jealously guarded by their witchy preceptor. They were enigmatic practitioners of the dark arts.

Seconds later, conversations rammed up. Everyone in the cantina had returned to revelry and carousing. The bar hummed with hard-edged and catchy tunes blasting out from the jukebox, blues numbers about hard drinking times and love gained and lost.

Eve remained stunned. She tried to sort through the shock of who she was seated next to, a man both cunning and genuine. He was edginess and bravado, sincerity and warmth. He scared her, an oasis concealing a venomous Rio Grande rattlesnake.

The rest of the men bragged. They boasted about being lawyers, offices about two blocks to the west, specialty criminal law. Suddenly, their look was not so much men on the prowl as professional scavengers. They bragged about their legal conquests.

A big case had been spread across the front page of the local newspaper, the *Aztlan Crier*. No one in town was unaware of the terrible doings of the defendant. The accused was loathed.

He had been indicted for verbally abusing then bludgeoning his wife to a bloody pulp of broken bones and smeared gray matter. For the *politico* of significant means, the evidence was hard and plentiful. He faced life in the infamous mid-twentieth century prison, Aztlan del Norte

State Maximum Security Penitentiary. The penitentiary had been built near the natural sandstone edifice dubbed The Devil's Throne. It was a realm of insolent and psychically contorted beings, known for extreme violence including beatings, rape, and murder.

Word from one end of the state to the other said he was guiltier than *el demonio*. No one doubted that the wheeler and dealer of politics, money, and mortality deserved to end his days locked up in one of America's most dangerous prisons.

The politico had been acquitted. Sam had taken on his case and won, to the chagrin of the district attorney and regional women's rights advocates. Spinning out one of the most spine- tingling, colorful, and compelling closing arguments ever uttered this side of the Sandia Mountains, Sam convinced the entire courtroom of the accused's innocence. Mesmerizing a jury, judge, news reporters, and public attendees, Sam Shear spun the tale of a man expertly framed by his deceased wife's ex-lover, a known philanderer and con artist.

Jury convinced, innocence assigned, the ex-lover stood up and darted toward the courtroom's back door. The sergeant-at-arms accosted him as he screamed wild-eyed and practically frothed at the mouth about the devil in the sharkskin suit. Dragged to the county jail, he awaited trial on charges of murder.

Formidable were Sam's abilities to undo the legal tangles of tarnished politicians, pimps, narcotics dealers, rapists, murderers, and thieves. There was a thrill to being with such a notorious fellow.

Research about dangerous warlocks ran through Eve's mind. The psychic antics of nasty warlocks set the world off-balance. Old mystical treatises said that chaotic energy powered a warlock's destructiveness. Sam was a lightning rod. Crises hit Sam the Arch Magus of downtown Aztlan del Sur and set his black magic crackling.

This kind of man danger was weird and delicious. Eve flushed with an edgy excitement. She fought against it, trying to hide the blush she sensed rippling over her face. It didn't work, as told by Sam's knowing glance out of the corner of his eye.

A psychology professor during her undergraduate years had taught that true insanity blended good and bad. It ensnared a person. There was just enough good to keep you in. There wasn't quite enough bad to make you leave. Eve was familiar with bad boys—and liked them—way too much.

Sam looked Eve's way with a boyish innocence.

Shirley bent Tanya's way then shook her head and spoke over the booze-spiked chatter, "So you're Sam the Man!" Her voice was raspy, deep-throated, and testy. Man-testy.

Sam smiled coolly. A perfect few seconds passed. "I'd never refer to myself that way." He squinted, permitted a tinge of embarrassment. It didn't fit.

"Then how would you refer to yourself, Mr. Lawyer?" Shirley's words were sharp and spicy.

Sam's colleagues let out a playful groan.

Plentiful libations always set Shirley off about men and needy egos. The vodka on the rocks supplied by her hot-and-bothered gent was gone. She'd drunk way more than she could remember on this mischief-ridden night.

Sam nodded as she ranted on. After a few choice cuts about every male being a boyish man, she pulled to a stop and eyed him with bloodshot intensity.

He lifted his hands. "Guilty as accused, Your Honor. But I gotta say, I'm just a guy trying to do my best." His blue eyes sharpened to a piercing cold.

Shirley didn't blink.

Eve cleared her throat and shook her head. Sam could smoothly cruise his way past any pothole. There was no curing a cocksure man.

Sam pulled back and stared at Eve. The flash of a hurt and exposed little boy scampered across his unlined face. Eve sometimes caught glimpses of the person beneath the persona, images from a scarred childhood. Then Sam's visage switched to a man who'd been wronged, jaws clenched, neck muscles taut. His look turned hard. It was as if he'd closed off his mind, a man well acquainted with the on and off switch of his humanity.

He sensed her dipping into vulnerable regions.

Eve's body tensed. She needed to get it together and leave. A man like this definitely could and would do a woman harm. She'd had to pull the plug on man-grief.

Sam sensed her intent and gently touched the top of her hand. Temper quelled, his features softened.

But best not to forget the guy switched on a dime. Mental instability up front and clear was redder than a red stop sign.

Sam caught the eye of the waitress. He lifted his chin. The waitress stopped where she was headed. She turned as though on command. At the booth, she looked at Sam, eyes mystified by her own abrupt compliance. He winked at her, patted her waist high enough for Eve to see he didn't go lower, and then ordered two more drinks, a single-malt scotch straight up and a vodka on the rocks. The waitress got lost in the pools of Sam's blue eyes, caught in a Sam-the-Man trance.

Robotically, she turned to walk off. Her skirt barely covered her curves. Sam gave a quick, predatory look. He cut his gaze and rolled his eyes back toward Eve. There was a perfect rhythm to it, Sam dangling his lingering eyes like bait, but not quite long enough for Eve to take the hook. There wasn't enough to comment about. Precision was his stock-in-trade, missteps unthinkable.

Eve slid her fingers across the table and remarked, "Whisky and vodka. Two-fisted drinker, huh?" Her voice was plain and loud, a bite on the tip of her tongue.

Sam grunted and shook his head. He drew a long breath then said, "Can't win with you, can I?" Naturalness and sincerity could seem real.

Eve didn't say a word. Time took too long to pass before the waitress delivered the drinks. Her hands trembled along the cheap, plastic serving tray, glasses rattling without spilling. She set the drinks down.

Sam shot Eve a sideways look and said, "Don't have to drink it." He looked down at the floor for a second; it spoke of dejection. He'd probably known testy women, had felt their bite. But the flip side of vulnerability was reactivity—temper.

Eve kept her guard high. She didn't want to set him off. He was ticking a little too loud, wound a little too tight. Hurt little boys in men's bodies could be rough. Eve snapped her fingers and broke Sam's spell, forcing the waitress's attention. "Take the vodka back, please."

Blood vessels alongside Sam's temples lifted and throbbed. He clenched his jaw, muscles distended. "Do as the lady says." He reached into his pants pocket and pulled out a money clip, flipping through the bills. He handed the waitress a crisp hundred and a twenty. "Paying up. Keep the change."

Eve stood to get past Sam. Everyone turned, quieted, and watched.

Sam leaned back so she could get by. He raised his hands. "I've met my match." The words were spat out like bad medicine.

Disgusted, Eve replied, "I'm nobody's match. Don't care to be." She walked toward the door.

Man-lure had been shiny. And shiny tarnished quickly.

He called out, "Well… wait a minute! Don't just leave me sitting here with my teeth in my mouth."

She didn't turn around. "Better teeth in mouth than not."

Hoots broke loose in the cantina like steers out of a corral. Laughter nearly drowned out the startup of the jukebox. Men slapped their thighs and pitched out whoops and hollers. Women let loose catcalls like feline creatures in heat.

The smudged glass door crept to a close. Eve came out from under the cantina's eaves into gusts of crisp, nighttime air washed clean by light autumn drizzles. The fresh high-desert night breathed sweet, cleansing out the cantina's stale fumes.

She knew the lair had been set, and she'd stepped in. Sam was more than a man looking to bed a woman. He'd already been with Eve and wanted more—not sex, her. He was way too intense and way too sure of himself. Everything in Eve wanted him, and everything in her said no and yes.

A lowrider cruised by on the narrow one-way street that shimmered with neon lights on wet asphalt. It was a 1962 four-door black Lincoln Continental, in perfect condition with an expensive and gleaming paint job, jacked up and pumping like a maddened iron beast. The tinted driver's side window was rolled down, shotgun pointing out. Gold-plated teeth grinned just as Sam the Man, the downtown lawyer, had grinned. Eve held her ground. Quick moves set off many a downtown, jacked-up grinner.

A vicious little gangster gave a quick wink and a nod then laughed and pulled his shooter back inside. Window rolling

up, the black sedan cruised on. A fiery painting of Tonatzé, Goddess of Aztlan, lay resplendent on the trunk.

Punk gangsters respected Tonatzé's enchantment and authority. They kept her close, didn't want to offend the Goddess. Girlfriends instructed their men not to go where they should not go or do what they should not do lest Tonatzé turned on them with serious *movidas*. The Goddess had *ways* and did what she did without warning.

Word flying down barrio streets had it that crossing Tonatzé would leave them in bad shape, without "junk in the trunk." Tonatzé was a life insurance policy, so downtown tough guys tried to stay close to the Goddess.

The car drove on for block after nighttime block and then popped out of sight into a shadowy ether sphere.

Eve waited for the cab she'd called. Colorful graffiti rose on either side of the two-story, brick walls flanking the alley. Street lamps on seventy-five-year-old crooked wooden poles lent a yellow radiance to the painted drama of a writhing man offered as a bloody sacrifice by Mayan priestesses.

Eve thought of the work she'd done on her backyard grotto. It was a ritual place to conjure the fearless energy of Tonatzé. An antique mirror was epoxied to the back of the sandstone grotto and reflected a black, foot-high stone sculpture of the Goddess.

A local carver had fashioned the statue from a small piece of marble, commissioned by Eve. The mirror for the grotto was obtained at a Saturday morning outdoor market. Old mirrors contained old energies, the seller claiming that it radiated an unearthly light on full moon nights. It had been in the possession of women adept in the supernatural and, allegedly, dated to sixteenth-century Aztlan.

The stone altar was used by Eve and company to conjure natural energies of earth, air, fire, and water. Tonatzé symbolized feminine strength and ancient powers. Around the altar, the four women entered mystic states with intuitive inspirations and visions.

The four mestizas frequently gathered at midnight, when the full moon shone most lustrously. They held hands, sipped their whiskeys, and inhaled magic herb. Soon the image of the Goddess flickered in rhythm with their soft singing under the light of the high-desert moon.

Chant and trance conjured natural magic. They yielded to relaxation, reverie, and trust in one another and the natural world. Descending into a meditative state, they were whisked from one world to the next.

On slips of paper, they quietly wrote their worries, dilemmas, trials, and tribulations. Seeking answers and relief, they placed the folded papers in a granite bowl before the altar. They lit a match. Paper burned. Silence wrapped its arms around the four. Gentle breezes stirred. Hoots of distant and nearby owls carried through the nighttime atmosphere.

Flames from the granite bowl rose three feet and abruptly expired, devoured by darkness. The ritual of fire fortified the coven, foul happenstance and unexpected hazard averted, all save one kind.

Man trouble waited for Eve like a demonic jack-in-the-box, head bobbing and grinning. Muscles up and down her back tightened. It was this that caused her to flee into denial, the thought of time wasted, mind and body pained. The desire to talk, confide in her friends about misgivings about

Sam, the last worst guy ever, fled like alley cats into a lonely night. Denial made everything go away—and stay gone—better than a couple of vodkas on the rocks on a chilly evening.

A white cab edged out of the alleyway bordering the cantina. It pulled stealthily alongside Eve. She bent down and looked through the smudged passenger window. She wanted to make sure she knew the cabbie. Past midnight was no time to be in a trusting mood. Grayish grime obscured her night vision, making it hard to see inside tinted windows.

The passenger's side window inched down. The cabbie wore a black leather cap. He leaned her way, smiled, and gave a nod.

"Hey, Gabriél. How's things crawling in the hood?" Eve opened the back door and got in, clicking her seatbelt.

Gabriél laughed. "Crawling, Professor. Always crawling." He didn't ask where she was going, simply sped off with a jolt.

Eve was a regular. Gabriél drove quickly and safely. Drizzle turned to rain that splattered furiously on the windshield, cold air gusting through car vents. Chills rippled up and down Eve's arms. She fought off troubling thoughts of Sam, the slick guy in the bar, the dark side of the sensitive lover of nights before.

"Hey, Professor," Gabriél spoke up, snatching Eve from her reverie. "Word on the street says it was a badass night at Los Muertos."

"What'd you hear?" Eve leaned back into the seat. She hoped Sam's foiled attempts to find her before this evening hadn't been carried to the wrong ears. Having a nasty-tempered lawyer tracking, stalking, and trying to make things right wasn't her idea of a wish come true.

"Guy was downed by a shard in the eye. Picked up by

paramedics. Docs diagnosed one thing. Ended up being more complicated. Piece of glass went into the brain. The fellow lost it. Dead. The old mirror, Professor, the old mirror."

Unnerved, Eve wrapped her arms around herself. She'd never known anyone who'd been killed by the legend. Now, she'd witnessed two deaths in less than a week. Both involved mirrors. Both were related to people she'd known or encountered. She sat lower in the torn, black vinyl seat, attention drifting to the radio, a song drifting out about loneliness, knowing yourself, and unexpected turns of fate.

CHAPTER 6

S weet Mary's thin bedroom wall vibrated to the thumping sound of hard rock and old blues blasting from the jukebox of Los Muertos Cantina. Tunes pounded through the night, vibrated along tips of peeling, faded green wallpaper.

Walking to the ancient lumpy bed, she spit on the soiled sheet. Rubbing hard to get up as much blood as she could, her fingertips heated. She stopped and kissed the burning flesh. Sweet Mary liked burning flesh almost as much as she liked bloodied flesh. Rubbing up a blood smear was a cherished ritual. The splotch of gunk was now brown, not red. It was an unholy end to an unholy deed.

She conjured a reputation far and wide, up and down Route 66. Never did she fail to live up to carnal expectations. Human flesh was her artistic medium. Sweet Mary smiled. She cut bloodied cloth out of the old sheet and placed it in an unsealed plastic baggie that gave off a musty smell.

There was a sharp knock at the door. Sweet Mary knew who banged on the flimsy piece of pine.

The old judge's blubbery ass and putrid emission lingered in her memory. Judge liked it hard. And Sweet Mary delivered harder. It was in the giving and taking of pain that men considered themselves men. They took, they gave, came back for more.

Sweet Mary patted the bag, giving it a final press, and zipped it to keep in the fresh and wet blood. Soon magic would be summoned. Terrible deities demanded fresh blood.

A lurid grunt came from behind the thin wooden door. Sweet Mary recognized the tone. She imagined the old judge quivering there, right hand grasping the peeled blue paint of the rotting wooden doorframe. The judge growled out he'd forgotten something. Deal was, though, he wanted something. He'd come back for another go with Sweet Mary.

But there were no two-for-one specials on this bruja's docket. Aztlan del Sur's major downtown witch never answered the door after customers had spurted and blown cumsoul juice. Mary's to take, Mary's to keep.

The bangs hit solid then brutal. "I know you're in there," the wheezing old fart ranted. He hung over six feet like a worm-eaten banana tree. His bent frame emphasized a stomach expanded way past nine months pregnant.

Sweet Mary didn't want him to have to cross her. She'd exercise a special kind of love. Cantankerous man turned into a puddle of piss was unsightly. And Sweet Mary could do much worse. Doling out afflictions was a special talent. Hemorrhoids and malignant tumors arrived and never stopped giving due to Sweet Mary's talents.

Simple as charcoal to cheap, white printing paper, Sweet Mary drew the likeness of the unfortunate fool. Puffs of black smoke coiled out to the white edges of curling paper. Desperation opened emotional doors. She spotted it in the man, drew from it in the man, had her way with the man.

She cherished the intonation that followed. *Bagabi laca lama sabathani. Bagabi laca lama sabathani. Bagabi laca lama sabathani.* It concentrated and directed the evil.

White paper jumped, a puff shooting up from underworld energies. And that was that, another foolish man, another wickedly productive day for Sweet Mary.

Initiation into the black arts had refined her talents. It taught Sweet Mary to morph men into forever-crazed mortals. Fear-ridden childhood nights in a religious orphanage with black-cloaked beings honed a girl's death instincts. It taught her to make men scream for an end to their miserable lives.

Local psychiatric hospitals, notably on full moon nights, were flooded with tales of *hombres locos* ranting about *la bruja mala*, the evil witch. They banged and banged and wouldn't stop banging their pulpy and bloody heads against white walls. Forlorn fellows never gained back their sanity.

Downtown alleys and West Mesa arroyos were littered with enfeebled souls scathed by the black magic of Sweet Mary. They clamored and ranted. Up one street and down the other, they raved to unseen presences about the evil witch of Aztlan del Sur.

Lard for brains banging on the door had no idea what lay in store for him if he got past the door and waddled his fat ass in Sweet Mary's quarters. He was used to doing damage and covering it easily as only a high-ranking judge could. A call, a wink, a favor done for a favor given, another working girl's complaint to metro police dismissed.

Complaints to city cops from abused women were no more than dirty tissues tossed into the stained and grungy trashcan at police headquarters. A special kind of love would cure the judge. He'd never inflict himself on another innocent female. Soon the city would wake up with a supernatural shock.

She envisioned the headline of the *Aztlan Crier* first spouting off the death of the loudmouthed fool in the bar. She could see it now, *Haunted Mirror Kills*! Then it would snap off another headliner in the metro section about the judge and the strangeness that overtook him. People wouldn't connect the two but Sweet Mary would.

And that's all that mattered—Sweet Mary and her satisfaction. Her evil ways never failed to pack jolts and shocks that left folks afraid to look in a mirror lest evil come their way. She salivated. The baggie and the blood would not go to waste.

Sweet Mary chuckled. *To hell with the fat-ass bastard. He got what he wanted and what he paid for.* Right up the ass, a twist and a turn from the heated toy.

The pounding on the door stopped. Silence.

It didn't last long. A final pound thudded hard. The middle door panel bent inward, wood slivers obtruding from the panel. Splinters poked up and out then the judiciary blubber huffed and puffed and departed. Stomp, stomp, stomp he went. The sound on the pavement was that of a lucky son of a bitch who was getting away with his hide, when it should have been peeled and nailed to a termite-infested telephone pole.

It would have been a bruja's personal treat to have topped a judiciary officer off with a slam jam that would have split his legal ass up the center and left him walking nice, slow, and obvious.

It would have served him right.

To Sweet Mary, one fool was like another. They were men. It began with a man, a black-cloaked man, Sweet Mary's black-cloaked man. He, dear old father, archbishop father, now long-gone father was no concoction of a little girl's mind.

Doctors said she made up bad memories because a bad father was better than no father. There was no record of her birth father, the certificate of birth absent a name. So, doctors asserted she kept bad and twisted memories rather than no memories.

The archbishop paid special visits to her in the orphanage, whispered in the ears of little Mary that she was his daughter as he stroked her hair and held her close. He visited the orphanage whenever he pleased. He preferred the dark of night when corridors were empty and other children slept.

He taught her what men were about. He started the love thing going. He was her father, the dear Archbishop of Aztlan. She learned that where there was a creed, there was no love. Religion killed. Sweet Mary was the offspring of religion gone bad.

Father and father's black-cloaked friends visited her as her reputation as a promiscuous beauty rippled through rectories. Father didn't know about the clerical underlings and their times with his daughter. He shouldn't have bragged. A little orphanage girl in the dead and cold of night did what a little girl did. She lay there in the steel bed of the orphanage run by nuns. She froze her body and mind, so went away, gone.

Body numb and mind gone, the little girl did not feel when so many black-cloaked men came and kept the love thing going so she would not be alone.

And now, it was Sweet Mary who was the wheeler and dealer in that special kind of love.

Sweet Mary sat with her elbows cocked against the lumpy mattress and watched the night roll on through the two-way mirror in her tight, little bedroom.

Music kicked into higher and louder gear. The three girlfriends were leaving with their nighttime pickups, fingers curling playfully around cheeks and necks. They wobbled their way out of the downtown meat market. Sam had gone his blustery way shortly after his new gal pal left him flustered and forlorn. The woman of Sam's fixation was also on her way, right into sordid surprises and concocted mischief.

Sweet Mary couldn't wait for the unfolding of wickedness to strike and take yet another targeting feline of the species down and out.

Another couple of quarters, and the night shot past ear-popping decibels that later morphed into headaches for the auditorily numb. One might have thought the scene of a bloodied eye and fat gent landing on his ample hindquarters would tone things down. No chance of mellowing for liars, fools, and desperate souls. They'd come out to forget, and they forgot quick as a switch of tunes on the shiny bright chrome-and-red jukebox.

Sweet Mary stood up from the dilapidated mattress. It had soaked up lives of forlorn and misbegotten beings. No more than five feet three, she tiptoed high enough to see most of her torso in the small, cracked bedroom mirror.

It hung askew over the dressing table, positioned in front of the queen-sized, rusty brass bed. Energy soaked in through the big mirror. Save for some needed touchups, she looked hot as an egg sizzling on a middle-of-the-summer Aztlan del Sur sidewalk.

Sweet Mary thrilled at her wickedly beautiful handiwork: tendons, muscles, and flesh. Shoulders up, present-moment adjustments were in order. Her platinum-blonde hair formed a tangled mess, sat like a rat's nest atop an otherwise curvaceous, lusty, and eternally youthful female body.

Sweet Mary didn't age. She hovered at twenty-seven years of age. Those closest to her—cultic associates she called them—never questioned. Gossipers said it was miraculous DNA.

Sweet Mary knew the power of man fluid. Energy flowed into recesses of the mind, aging crevices of body, muscles, cell membranes, skin texture invigorated. Extracting vigor and essence from patrons, and leaving the worst, was pure art. Taking it was easy as a master pickpocket sights and swipes, no one the wiser.

Through the ages, certain women knew of such dark arts. Women of hideous secrets and ages-old black magic led the unsuspecting into inescapable lairs. They killed with an intense stare at vulnerable prey. They pulled out and ate a still-beating heart without so much as a gasp from the victim, devoured leg muscles with no more than a lingering mental focus, the tortured victim watching, unable to scream.

As seductress, Sweet Mary bewitched males. Longingly, they yielded body, mind, and soul to the black magic witch. In exchange, they were conferred sexual ecstasy. Then they paid up.

She'd learned from the best, the old witches of the north, after having indulged her evil side in a delicious atrocity.

Upon her fourteenth birthday, she had been secretly escorted by six nuns to the archbishop's hacienda. He was to raise her as his niece. Six months later, the archbishop was discovered in bed, dead, his still-tumid cock severed and bundled at the root.

It was stuffed into his mouth, the words, As You Give So You Receive, carved across his naked belly by the shard of a mirror propped against the stiff member. The shard reflected his tortured face. The gashes were outlined with red lipstick. Household staff confirmed the archbishop forced the child to wear the hideous color to accentuate her full lips.

Little Sweet Mary disappeared. Local media reported she had been kidnapped by the archbishop's murderer. The wealthy church quashed investigations into the hideous crime. Clerics knew the evil tale behind the murder and of course said nothing.

Clerics fantasized about capturing her. They bragged in clandestine cleric meetings that "doing it to a witch, an archbishop's foul offspring" would be an incomparable delight.

Committed to cleansing and ridding their land of witches, a cleric would draw a large circle in the desert sand. Standing there, he would perform exorcisms. One time, a braggadocio, foul-breathed priest by the name of Father Roberto stood inside the circle, his shirt inside out to repel evil. Reputedly, witches, who came his way and shape-shifted into coyotes, would be trapped in the center of the circle. Once caught, they'd morph into a haggard woman who withered and died.

Father Roberto never should have confronted the ultimate female force, a woman of nightmarish magic.

Sweet Mary forthrightly stepped into the circle, planted a juicy kiss on the gawking man of the cloth's dry lips, and quicker than a rattler hisses and strikes, the earth cracked and opened up around him. Father Roberto, fool that he was, wide-eyed and screeching, tumbled into the Abyss of the Witches.

The Abyss of the Witches was known throughout Aztlan del Norte and del Sur. It was the underworld region of no return. Lost souls and damned beings forever haunted its frigid atmosphere. Present day, it lay near Sweet Mary's apartment in downtown Aztlan del Sur, a surreal realm transposed from place to place depending on need and circumstance.

Aztlan railed against the witchy women, the sorceresses of the flesh. In quiet moments of desperation, when the evil winds of brujas felled trees and ripped tin roofs off and away like blown trash, awestruck townspeople and rural folk alike blessed themselves. With shaky hands, they desperately beseeched their god to ward off the powers of *Las Brujas Malas* and Michté, doing business as the one and only Sweet Mary.

Sweet Mary loved the old witches. As a child, she'd absconded with witches of the north. Their dreams led them to the gifted child. They guided her in what to do to the clerical prick on his customary night of "special caretaking." Sweet Mary had learned from the best.

She reached a stiffened hand to the dresser below the mirror, stroking a chipped and discolored black resin figurine. She had a statuette of Michté, Queen of the Dead, fashioned from dried and cured bat dung that clung to the walls of the Abyss of the Witches.

She turned her gaze to the cracked bedroom mirror. Black circles, wrinkles of times, age spots suddenly clustered over otherwise porcelain skin. She hissed and snarled. Sweet Mary whispered desert *Sabbat* prayers, "*Bagabi laca lama sabathani. Bagabi laca lama sabathani. Bagabi laca lama sabathani.*" Chanting grew fierce. The voices of Las Brujas Malas resounded in her ears. Inner heat intensified. Skin, pores, muscles, and sinews burned white hot.

Her body quivered at the thought of the witches who'd taught her the art of seducing and using. She'd seduced men who pranced and paraded, the most vulnerable. A deliciously easy score for a skilled vixen. Obvious strut—weak man.

Violence shook through her body, beads of perspiration trickling down her temples. Her fingertips grew cold. Hands clenched into fists. She remembered the men, black-cloaked men, strutters.

The room, the world, her mind spun and rocked uncontrollably as a child, and then as an adult. Sweet Mary's eyes rolled back into her head, and the world faded away as she slumped back into her bed and spun down into the Abyss of the Witches.

CHAPTER 7

Gales of wind force swept up from the Abyss of the Witches. Sweet Mary tumbled into the realm of dreams and nightmares. It fomented with unsettling images of tortured souls, bodies twisted, burned, plucked, and spoiled under the name of the Ecclesia Dei.

Religion damaged humankind and Michté thrived. Appalling odors under the earth penetrated the limestone walls of the abyss. It was the stink of love gone bad. She smelled the stench, savored its wildness. Repugnant smells betrayed the presence of evil. She inhaled and sighed.

She tumbled and tumbled and tumbled downward at a speed that plastered her hair across her cheeks. Irritating gales intensified the force and mocked the soothing sounds of the Wind Temples of Quetzalcoatl, Mesoamerican feathered serpent deity, boundary maker between earth and sky.

Spirals of stained limestone and discolored granite ridiculed the purity of Quetzalcoatl's temple. Chipped, coiling conch shells forming the wicked chasm, the Abyss of the Witches mocked the great Goddess of Aztlan, Tonatzé.

She was the Goddess of the Wild Thing, deity of inestimable influence. Hers was a might unassailable, save by those whose love had been scorned and whose hatred brewed potent and blasphemous.

From the Abyss of the Witches, a high-pitched sound cracked through the atmosphere, limestone dust trickling from overhead. Dust flew this way and that as Sweet Mary twisted side to side on her furious descent. It was the howling of subterranean beasts, souls of the forsaken. Torment fueled the rage of Las Brujas and Sweet Mary, preceptor and guide.

Wind streams jettisoned through a multitude of caverns, depthless black holes in the sides of the walls. God-awful vibrations set in motion a crumbling of rocks. The sides of the haunted abyss threatened to collapse.

The hellish pitch racked through Sweet Mary's ears, the force nerve damaging. But she was no mere mortal that needed to cover her ears from risk or fear. She let the unwholesome energy spike its way up her spinal cord up and brain, crackling with electricity and manic vitality. Her body shook with delight. Waves of white-hot power and searing light tore across her corneas, the pain titillating. She moaned blissfully as her body shuddered and the speed slowed.

Finally, the delightful and hellish fall and din ceased. She stood at the black, gaping, earthen mouth of her ancestors. She was unshaken. The fall was a familiar deepening by which she accessed kindred female spirits of malevolent arts. They encircled her, dozens of screeching, sharp-toothed wraiths, blood dripping from the corners of their mouths. Furious winds whipped up from beneath the ground and spun Sweet Mary and fellow specters through the air like wind-tossed feathers.

Suddenly, she desired to waken. She hoped to open her

eyes in her bedroom before hitting the ground. The ground hurt, cracked her legs, spine, and skull. The fall would come, and there was no way to escape it.

With horrendous force, Sweet Mary hit the ground. Feet snapped. Femurs shattered. Spine cracked. Neck snapped. Skull was pulverized. Yet the mind hovered. Waves, particles, atoms swiftly reconstructed. Body rematerialized, unscathed.

She was on her feet. She held her head high. She was Michté.

Centuries of voices of despoiled women wept and cried out from the gray and green granite walls of the ancestors, whose spirits plastered this horrifying region. Deceased souls of women in Michté's lineage, those used and abused by men with black cloaks or slick suits and wily ways, clung to the shadows and howled and screamed. Blackened earth beneath her feet shook.

Rage fueled Michté and the cult of Las Brujas Malas. It made for an unwholesome magic that flickered with blue currents of electric energy, whipping through space and time that encircled Michté and propelled her up, out of the twilight realm.

Three more times, she repeated the cultic verse, "*Bagabi laca lama sabathani. Bagabi laca lama sabathani. Bagabi laca lama sabathani.*"

Her mind completed the ascent. She was back in the waking world. Quickly, she reoriented to space-time reality, the descent and ascent familiar. She stroked the black statuette of Michté. As she wafted the unholy fumes of centuries-old sulfuric gases into her nostrils, the figurine continued to steadily emit wisps of gray smoke.

Without the journey into the abyss, conjuring was weaker. Entering the old place strengthened the magic. It came as a foul-smelling gas. Sweet Mary waited for her vision to fully adjust. The descent and ascent happened in seconds, human senses slow to adapt. Her head spun from the smell, the momentary nausea passing, and dizziness settling as the hallucinogenic vapors took their effect.

Reality shifted. Her apartment appeared far off, miles away and tiny then grew close, surrounded her. All was well. She yawned, smiled contentedly, and stretched. Proudly, she gazed into the small, cracked mirror in the dank and putrid room.

Never was her petition to Michté denied. Homage had been rendered; youth returned to full luster. The raccoon was gone. In its place was flawless porcelain skin, blue eyes bright, platinum-blonde hair, thick and coiffed.

But hunger would return. Old miens would come a-haunting. Raccoons quickly got hungry. They would scavenge. Bellies demanded satiation. Pure and porcelain white cried out for sustenance. Needy men stood at the ready—nutrition for bottom feeders.

The telephone's incessant ringing snapped Sweet Mary's mind fully back to reality. Renewed intensity and fury were hers. Remembrance of unholy things stirred unholy passions. She burned hot with the black magic of Las Brujas.

Sweet Mary wanted to sizzle the phone wires with her mind. She did not. Empowered by the horrid Abyss of the Witches, she could do far more than burn wires. She could set fire, loosen, and project lethal shards. Directing a malicious thought someone's way, an evil feeling, a nasty attitude, and out would crawl a stroke of very bad luck.

The phone did not stop ringing. Disgustedly, she picked up the old receiver. The cracked, black plastic barely hung together. She held it by her fingertips. Silence hung in the air like a dead man in a noose. A smile crawled over her face. She knew who it was. She recognized the breathing. She waited for him to speak.

He spoke with starts and fits. "Mary... I... I... I'm coming up. We gotta... ttt-talk." After the briefest hesitation, he slammed the phone down.

It was Sam. She hated pitiful Sam. She loved pitiful Sam. He exuded a bluster that others feared, but Sweet Mary knew of Sam's bravado, had birthed Sam's bravado.

Odd, Sam never stumbled when it came to words. Something had hold of him. It should prove both fascinating and temporary.

Sweet Mary loved twists and turns in the life of Sam Shear, the lawyer written about by newspapers as the *Archmagus of Aztlan del Sur*. They portended things colorful and dastardly. They provided Sweet Mary with dastardly entertainment. She knew the rancorous origins of the man and his story.

Sweet Mary couldn't help but love the tough guy. He was nothing but an empty heart, fried mind, and dead soul. His psychic innards had long been sucked out. He didn't blink. Guys who didn't blink were gone—there was no one there. Sam was gone, no one there, no one left.

Opponents thought he'd mastered an art form. They couldn't discern his thoughts or feelings. Alas, Sam had no soul.

Sweet Mary had fashioned many men, yet Sam stood out as her sterling example of malleability and cunning. Since young manhood, after graduating from law school, he had listened and learned at the knee of Sweet Mary. Sam soaked up Sweet Mary's teachings as doughnut dough sopped up grease. He excelled in manipulation and tormenting peers. Translated, he was one hell of a criminal lawyer.

Sweet Mary by his side, Sam morphed into a man with a piercing, soulless gaze, ruthless ambition, and coldhearted ways. He didn't blink. He didn't feel. He had nothing to blink or feel with. Sweet Mary had it.

Sam looked straight ahead and, easy as bird shit plopping and spreading thick as goo on glass, he made a person believe what he wanted them to believe. There was no leaning on facts of law for Sam the Man. He was his own brand of law and his own type of reprehensible abrogado.

Juries and judges fell under his indisputable spell. Early on, he had been a lawyer of no standing; then he learned psychic, back-door antics and black magic artifice from the one and only Sweet Mary of downtown Aztlan del Sur.

Sweet Mary sat on the bed and took a deep swallow of pride. Sam was the goddamn fiercest criminal lawyer this side of the Rio Grande. She was proud.

Common hustlers of the law slithered up and down streets and back alleys; the best aligned their wills with nefarious families or power-wielding corporations. They were barristers of ill will and formidable repute, dynamite in the courtroom, replete with gutter rat snarls and bites inflicted via arguments that'd make a rabid dog look like an elementary school hamster in a cage.

They were made men of the routine variety.

The difference came when Sweet Mary made the man. Sweet Mary made Sam. No badass Mafia or war chest, stocked legal corporation behind this man. Badass Mafia and deep-pocketed firms weren't needed with Sweet Mary around. She sported in the conjuring and tutoring of trickery that left mafiosi and corporations dumbfounded and utterly slack-jawed.

Sam knew not to forget the creatrix of his lawyerly mojo

and personal fortune. In return, Sam watched over Sweet Mary's concerns. Magic occasionally couldn't get past the law. Sam could and did.

Nothing could happen to Sam. Sweet Mary's black bag of magic tricks fortified his sharp-tongued antics. Tides of legal events conspicuously turned in Sam's ever-grateful direction. On and on, evil worked its spellbinding mojo. A judge's decision would slam against the tide of voter opinion, and a pernicious lawsuit would be thrown out of court.

There was the time an entire squadron of opposing attorneys took up and disappeared. Remains of the blathering bunch were located months later. Decomposing remainders putrefied in a lone mountain cabin. A few teeth in each mouth had been left for identification.

Sweet Mary's attention lit on her classic German pocketknife. The knife sported a three-inch blade. She removed it from her expensive Florentine leather purse. The expertly honed blade gleamed with dark radiance in the dimly lit room.

She retrieved the sealed plastic baggie from the nightstand drawer and opened it. It was wet, perfect. She cut an end off the patch of blood-soaked sheet.

Mary had her ways of keeping those who needed to be kept. The judge was such a one. His mind was of the teetering-tottering variety. Keeping the blood kept the man. Fresh blood smoothed old bones. During nightly black magic keeping rituals, blood was smeared into the skin by witches up and down the Rio Grande. It smoothed away the ravages of time, restored vitality. One nightly smear vanquished years of depletion and decay or topped off a salubrious incantation.

Sweet Mary decided on a little top-off to an otherwise memorable replenishment of female witchery and vigor.

Blood of children was preferable. It gave her back what she had lost as innocence bequeathed eye-popping luster to skin tone and tightened any sagging. The middle-aged and older were good for a quick pop, a little touch-up as a post-incantation formality.

Sweet Mary had once been young and delicious. Decades of witchcraft antics took an infernal toll. But now, this witch's skin sported a better-than-new glow. Nothing like a trip to the Abyss for a black magic infusion. A final touch of fresh blood vanquished a few hair-thin wrinkles.

Sam was getting older. He fretted about it. He asked, pled actually, for the virility of former years. He was nearly fifty. So, out of the traces of kindness of her sordid little heart, Sweet Mary gave Sam regular jolts of sexual magic with a fresh blood chaser that revved up libido and kept a wanton man wanton. That made him more kept than he already was. Sweet Mary didn't let on about this, figured she'd leave in a little bit of his foolish ornery and arrogance; otherwise, he'd know he was in the process of being kept for good.

Little by little, a man was taken, and then kept, and then kept permanently. Kept forever.

Sweet Mary had to be watchful. She couldn't chance Sam catching on. He'd fight being totally under her spell. It'd ruin things between them. He still had some will inside him. She'd left it there. It was called ornery. If she sapped it away, he'd know it. If she kept going slowly, Sam would soon be a good and obedient boy, never tempted by bouts of ornery. He'd be forever by Sweet Mary Mama's side. Then there'd be no way out. Sam the Sweet Mary Made Man would be hard or limp according to her dictates. He'd know it, he'd fully know it.

So for now, she left some ornery in.

A wry smile overtook her full lips, a long red streak

sculpted across exquisitely high cheekbones. Age had now faded like the last traces of dust after a spring rain. Black magic had shot its wonder-working luster through blood and bones and sinew and skin. The sordid woman of eternal youthfulness in the mythopoeic land of Aztlan del Sur was without peer. She did what she wanted, when she wanted. It pleased her. She waited for Sam, the Sweet Mary Made Man.

Jittery sounds of a key in a shaky hand slid around the brass deadbolt on the outside door.

Sam must've figured that by midnight, it'd be locked. Downtown streets crawled with creepers.

Sam never knocked. And Sam never shook. Something bad had bitten and torn a juicy chunk of hide from the ruthless lawyer of Aztlan del Sur. He'd never been like this, so not himself, so ripe for Sweet Mama Mary.

She swallowed hard. This was going to be a good time, a fine time for Sweet Mary to love Sam as she always did, in the way he needed it. She loved him not as a woman with a man but as a mother soothing her son. In a shaky mood, Sam was like a starving feral dog that'd been beaten. Only she could handle the unpredictable and high-tempered fool.

The key kept up an incessant scratching, and the man, a pitiful cursing barely muffled and terribly indicative of waning abilities. Sweet Mama Mary imagined Sam walking through the door all psychically scraggly and whipped. He'd be edgy. Mean edgy.

She threw the covers over the bed. No one was to see the under layer. No one was allowed to see the hallowed, well-worn sheets. People knew, men surmised and fantasized, but only payees were allowed entrance to the intimacies of the sorceress' bed. All the rest secretly wondered what it was like in between the infernal layers of carnal delights. It was Sweet Mary's bed. It was Sweet Mary's to know.

Every morning she bundled the sheets and left them on the floor, maids instructed to pitch them into a specially appointed incinerator in the basement of the old brick building. They'd been cautioned to maintain this secret ritual under the severest of consequences. Sweet Mary ordered it, eyes unmistakably terrifying.

No one was the wiser as to why an incinerator was marked for one person and one task. Only one housekeeper had ever countered the mandate. That was not so wise for one who found herself spontaneously aflame in the basement of the old brick building. She had been stuffed into the incinerator as by the hand of an invisible deity, blackened, dead, ash remains disposed of in an outside dumpster.

Finally, the door clicked open and in walked Sam. His presence gave her a thrill. It fueled her with loathing and pity, and a power that let him know she was the dominant one in this dance.

He squinted, cursed a few feeble words as his eyes adjusted to the dimness of the accursed sanctuary. Sweet Mary despised light, bright or dull, and so turned lumens down to traces of misty gray. Sam always needed time to adjust to changes, whatever shifts of time, person, or place Sweet Mary set in motion. She was always churning and burning situations, people, and relationships.

Tonight, she'd left all lights off save the low-watt red from the bathroom and the dim green of the table lamp near the front picture window that was covered by greasy and stained cream-colored curtains. She liked the red, blue, and green neon lights that lit up bars and clubs up and down the street. She let the neon flickers and shafts in through cracks and slim openings in the curtains and space between warped wooden door and jamb.

Sam didn't try to turn on the floor lamp near the door, the brightest in the squalid little room. Light was nothing Sam liked either. Eyes simply needed time. He let out a sigh and the huff of a dazed and confused man.

Poor Sam.

What was Sweet Mary going to do with a guy she wanted to churn and burn this instant? Up in flames he'd go, right there on the spot into a little pile of ashes that could be swept up and dumped. She'd done it before, no trace, no DNA, not a whit of human aftermath to sully her otherwise pure abode.

She hated weakness, sighs, huffs. Weak men. Poof and he'd be gone.

She decided not to. "Took you long enough. Where were you? Havin' a shot with the old judge, or what was left of him once I left him dried up and spent?"

Sam didn't laugh. He stood there like an erect corpse. This wasn't the feared downtown barrister, wordless, a strain in his eyes reminiscent of the old days of a near-gone and soul-lost man.

Sweet Mary didn't break the silence. She let quiet do what it did and come back to her. Listening to its message was a skill she'd learned from the old witch preceptors up north.

In the dark of moonless desert nights, they told a young girl to listen to the silence in the presence of distraught men. In it, lay the essence of the man. Silence held the message of what a man was made of and what could be done with him.

Forlornly, Sam sat down on the bed beside her. She hated

this, hated the forlorn and therefore pathetic male beside her. It turned her wicked stomach. Again, she thought of ending this tomfoolery of a pity party. She patted her hand on the saggy mattress, and Sam nestled closer. He hung his head, shoulders twitchy, black locks curling toward his eyebrows. His skin was grayish, fingers trembling slightly, skin clammy.

He was no feral creature. He looked like a beaten-down and slump-shouldered *viejito*. Old men made Sweet Mary's skin crawl, blood curdle, and bile surge up her windpipes. Sweet Mary's fury welled. Seeing a made man like Sam stooped was like gazing into a toilet full of day-old vomit. Nonetheless, she stayed quiet and fought back biliousness and temper. For one reason only, could Sam get so damnably down and unconscionably low.

No rival, enemy, or villain dragged Sam into the outhouse shitter like a fine-looking thing with a hot way and a sizzling platter of goods that he couldn't get his hands on.

Sam turned and looked up at Sweet Mary, forlorn and pathetic.

Sweet Mary wanted to slap him, and then do the thing she ached to do. She simply would point a finger, paralyze him by this well-practiced act, and then focus at her brow point till it burned red hot. The weak man Sam would be up in smoke and *poofed* away, gone. However, Sweet Mary had invested too much energy on this one to let him go. Still, it was sickening to have spent precious vim, vigor, and petrifying dynamism of the most feared witch of downtown Aztlan del Sur on such an easily woman-whipped little bitch of a man.

Sam picked up on her nasty vibe and put his head back down, this time cupping his palms against tear-streaked pink cheeks. Slapping him would be too good for one who couldn't face his hard-hearted mentor and look his mean-spirited majesty in her totally judgment-ridden face.

He blurted out, "She chewed me up and spit me out."

Sweet Mary's hand was itchy. One good slap and he'd be out, wouldn't know what had happened when he woke up facedown on the cum-spotted carpet. She should do that; he deserved it. He needed to be hurt. Men needed to be hurt. It welled. The desire burned fiercely. Her face reddened. She'd grind her heel into the back of his neck near the brain stem, and then pop it in until it snapped off, and Sam popped out of existence. But it'd be too good for him. He needed to face up and fess up.

That's where Sweet Mary came in. Her heart began to soften. She let the sympathy in. She always got something out of the deal when she put a little more into it with Sam. Pathetic bastard would be just a little more loyal, bonded, soldered. Sam gave her the chance to again prove her mettle. She had what it took to raise the dead — or in this case, near dead — to life.

She stroked the back of his neck. The brain stem was a delicate thing that controlled life and could indeed be pierced, escorting one deplorable life out of this realm of existence. Fingers then hand trembled a smidgen. She refrained, energy mitigated, for Sweet Mary had her own kind of reasonable heart. "Talk to me, honey." Sweet Mary always said, "Talk to me, honey" when she meant, "Feed me your pain."

"She got to me. Bad." Sam quivered. The man wasn't taken aback in the slightest by his ever-so-obvious feebleness. A scintillating opportunity had presented itself to Sweet Mary.

Wicked joy shot through her psychic veins, akin to mainlining high-dose caffeine through an early morning bloodstream. She loved the shiver of it. Intense man-pain made opiates seem like pink bubble gum. Goose bumps rippled then tumbled from head to toe and curled into muscles, tendons, and arteries. Sweet Mary loved the quickening and shudder that came with man-pain.

The warmth between her legs grew blistering. She let it blister. Wetness followed. It was delightful. Sweet Mary stroked Sam's head. It was all in the stroking, always in the stroking for men. Stroking gave and took then stopped when the getting and taking had been done.

"She brought trouble. Made my mind hurt." He squeezed his temples with his palms before looking up again. "But I want her." He breathed hard.

Sweet Mary's palm itched about as bad as a witchy woman's could, but she held back so he'd go on. And he went on, over every excruciatingly raw and minute detail of what had transpired with a downtown bar bitch. Stroking and more stroking.

He ended with, "I need to follow up." He'd gotten stuff off his chest. He was back to himself after venting and dumping.

Stroking and more stroking. Energy and more energy. Giving and giving. Sweet Mary got Sam where Sam needed to be.

Still, he wasn't at his mean-spirited and high-minded man best. Sweet Mary had fashioned him to be and stay that way. He'd been a challenge and was one now. He knew to let everyday nasty women pass—to use them, leave them, set fire to their memory. But at least for right now, his teeth and grit had returned. They set hard across Sam's chiseled face.

Stroking and more stroking.

"Why not put one of your PIs on her?"

"No... I'll tend to her." He shrugged her hand off his head

and shoulders. A quiver went through him. She noticed it by the quiver and shudder, a millisecond of a climax. It always ripped through him when Sweet Mary's black magic power, the stroking got him back to Sam the Sweet Mary Made Man.

Stroking complete.

"My guys went with her friends. They'll get me leads. Then I'll juice 'em and target." He smiled. The look was predatory like a shadow-hidden rattler set on a tiny puppy. Mischief was back and had grabbed hold hard and yanked. Full throttle it was. Sam was a hundred percent back. Thanks be to Michté, Sweet Mary's work hadn't been in vain. She took fearsome pride in her most dastardly creation.

Sam stood up, the blood flow flushing his face a radiant crimson with a protruding temple throb. Expertly, he adjusted his linen shirt, the folds and wrinkles magically disappearing. He swept back his black hair, fingers hovering a millimeter over the strands. Filaments obeyed, lay back, sheened down to perfect. Shoulders adjusted and head high, he appeared to hover in Sandia Mountain heights with deities infinite and infernal.

"Thank you." He nodded with a glance then turned and left. There was no door slamming. He closed it nice and quiet.

Sweet Mary had raised a gentleman, conniving, nefarious, dashing. Her heart swelled with pride. All was once again perfect in the world of transmogrifying realities and foul things set on course. Things were as they should be.

The knife gleamed on the nightstand. Taking hold of it, Sweet Mary twirled it across her fingers skillfully. She flipped it closed. A quick toss landed it in her purse.

Sweet Mary had her black magic mojo, her looking-glass shards, her quickened energy to spark blazes, and her gleaming tungsten blade.

Abruptly, she left the dingy sacral quarters, malicious intent whipping through her mind like high-desert mountain wildfires.

CHAPTER 8

Worry gnawed at Eve like earthworms burrowing through her early morning downtown garden. She sat at the back of the cab and thought about garden earth, wet from mildew and light rains the night before. They reminded her of things she looked forward to, and hoped one day to return to, once the horror of Graciela's death eased and she found, and perhaps even settled into, love.

What a thought it was—love. Her hopes never seemed to die, buffeted by disappointment and trod under by men of calloused heart. But something within her went on. Perhaps it was all for nothing, but then maybe not. It was the "maybe not" part that she was willing to lean into and move forward with.

Eve wasn't looking forward to being alone at home, walking into a dark house, no one there to greet her and warm her bed. The thought of the empty bedroom and cold bedsheets sent a shiver up her spine. There were people who had love, someone to be there, waiting for them to come home.

She decided she didn't want to go straight home, so she asked Gabriél to drive for a while along the deserted dirt road bordering the Rio Grande. "Let's go there, Gabriél. I think I'll ask you to wait for me. I'll take a short walk and air out my mind."

By his silence and his quick glance at her through his rearview mirror, she could tell he was concerned.

She reassured him. "No problem, Gabriél. I'll stay close, just need to get a little fresh air near the river by the cottonwoods." The thought of going there, away from the hum of city nightlife, eased her shoulder muscles. She breathed a little easier.

She looked out the window of the cab as they made their way down Central Avenue and drove past Rio Grande Boulevard, coming close to the river entrance near the Aztlan del Sur Botanical Garden. "I love the smell of cottonwood leaves as they turn yellow, some of them already fallen. It takes me back somehow to childhood on the pueblo."

Her mind further relaxed with the soothing memories before tightening quickly with the cold remembrance of a mother lost in her own loveless life. Of a father, a man no more than traces of memory, a black and hooded figure in the night who came, went, and soon was no more.

Gabriél remained quiet and listened, always ready to lend his understanding ear.

So she continued, "There's a sadness to fallen leaves, you know. The chill of the autumn air, the dark of night, yellow leaves strewn along the riverbanks. There's a sadness there. The atmosphere and earth breathe with it." Tears welled; she did not fight the grief.

Fighting feelings, stuffing them had practically become an art form. It was relieving when she didn't do it. *You're a*

tough one, Eve. You want to do things your way. It is your path.
Graciéla smiled from the recesses of her mind and tender
heart space.

As they approached the botanical garden's parking area,
Graciéla's presence was so near, she could have been sitting
beside Eve in the cab. Eve startled, practically hearing her
voice next to her. *Do not yield to despair. It breeds weakness.*

Graciéla had often repeated this cautionary teaching over
afternoon tea. She didn't want Eve to succumb to the dark
pull of desperate souls. Intuitively, she sensed that a hidden
despair was Eve's constant companion, taunting and teasing
her from behind a locked cage, wanting attention, feeding that
comes from worry and yielding to dark thoughts. A
childhood of neglect and misfortune on the pueblo had
birthed Eve's plight. Her father had indeed been no more than
a passing shadow. Darkness cloaked him. There then gone.

Her mother's abandonment bred a bitter loneliness. Each
day at their tiny adobe pueblo home, she hoped her husband
would return and stay. He did not. It was the custom of the
men of Aztlan to have their women, to go about their wiles
without regard for progeny or love. And so, men became no
more than shadows passing in the night.

There had been no way out of hard times and terrible
sadness as a child. It became an infection, the twist and turn
of a loveless life passed on from mother to daughter.
Psychologists spoke of generational trauma, the passing on of
familial injury, pain, and loss. Eve slumped back momentarily
in the seat of the cab.

Gabriél pulled into a parking area beneath a stand of
centuries-old cottonwoods. He turned off the engine and
stayed quiet. He was used to Eve and her silent reflections.
She stared out into the dark and saw moonlight dance across

the Rio Grande. It reminded her of herself as a little girl watching the river pass from the tarnished window of her pueblo home. She had learned to go to a dark corner of mind and watch things go by.

Sometimes, the mood would pass. Other times it wouldn't, but simply watching things go by helped. A little girl witnessing the coming and going of all things. Whispering ghosts called to her. They were specters in the night surrounding the car, coming in close. They had told her as a young child to let go and die, to cease living.

Eve stepped out of the car. The specters dissipated. Graciéla whispered, *Life is a dream, despair a waking nightmare*. Memories of an old witch cursing her from behind the mirror at the cantina flittered through Eve's mind. She flinched. She shook her head, didn't want to think about it. She shoved away the lingering energies of the ghosts and the witch.

She looked around the deserted area. Gabriél watched through the rearview mirror. Without him near, she wouldn't feel safe alone in this isolated area. Coyotes howled like babies wailing in the night.

Cottonwoods, sprawling Spanish olive trees, and rows of scrub oak lent ample hiding for dangerous characters. Overhead branches, sharp and crooked, loomed with shadows across dusty paths winding deep into North America's largest cottonwood forest. The voice of a woman weeping for her lost children were haunted legends paired with this eerie land.

She got back in the cab and asked Gabriél to drive up a bit more to the area between the cattle-guarded entrance and the exit that swooped near a bordering barrio.

He drove ahead then pulled over to the spot she'd requested. "I'll go with you, Professor."

"No, Gabriél. I won't go far." She had to be alone.

Gabriél insisted once more as she got out of the taxi and started to walk toward the dark *bosque*. When Eve didn't reply, he opened his door and leaned over the top of his car as she walked into the forest. "Okay, Professor, I know how you are. I'll wait right here."

She looked back, nodded, and smiled.

Gabriél suddenly seemed unusually tall, commanding, casting an otherworldly glow, perchance from the light of the full moon. His eyes were luminous. He was a good friend, a comfort especially when nighttime pressed and risk felt close at hand. There were good men in the world, she assured herself. Gabriél was one. He'd come into her life for a reason. He turned up when she needed him, his presence protective, comforting.

She called out, "Thank you, Gabriél! You're my guardian angel."

"One of many, Professor. One of many."

Gabriél stood beside his cab and watched with his arms folded as the professor disappeared amid ancient cottonwoods, guardians of the river realm. The white spot between his eyes warmed. It was deemed the third eye to mystic mortals. To those of Gabriél's ilk, it was a spiritual faculty always at the ready.

As through a glass, he saw a wicked woman fueled by rage. She projected fury. Gabriél quickened to her identity. Michté's eyes targeted Eve. Fury was her stock-in-trade. She hated women such as Eve, those who could love.

Gabriél saw into the distance, miles away to the West Mesa of Aztlan del Sur. Michté and her terrifying display of energy, as though on cue, spun across the open swath of desert. She appeared as a spinning orb of fire, a huge tumbleweed with a blackened center radiating red and white-tipped flames. It burst into pure energy, disappeared then rematerialized and continued along its furious path. The land was scorched with its heat. A charred path trailed the wheel of fire.

It was a message to Gabriél, one long known by both angelic dominions in the world of light and devilish powers in the legions of hell. Gabriél looked away, folded his arms, watchfully waiting for Eve as she walked along the bosque path.

Eve slowly made her way along the ghostly trail, snaking a dusty path down to the riverbank. High-pitched coyotes and rustling among the brush didn't lessen her resolve. She needed to see past the night's confusion and edginess. Clearing out tension and the pull to dark places of her mind needed to be done before going home and descending into the realm of sleep and dreams.

Her dreams had been plentiful as of late. They'd become more intense. More nights than not, she'd awoken in a sweat, heart racing, surrealistic images swirling and lingering. Minutes passed before she transitioned from the dream world, her mind inebriated with symbols and images ceaselessly tugging and warning.

Last night, she bolted up, a woman's hands gripping her

throat. In the nightmare, she jumped out of bed and went to her living room where she thought she'd heard an intruder. Banging at the front door and a clanging of pots and pans in the kitchen were vivid and loud. She'd felt fear and anger; no one was going to violate the boundaries of her abode. She knew how to protect herself and would. From behind, a woman's hands encircled her throat and squeezed.

The nightmare had faded. She opened her eyes. The fingers around her neck lessened their tension. She touched her neck. There were no fingers, no hand, no one in her bedroom.

Startling dreams, she'd learned from Graciéla, spoke of truth breaking into consciousness. Something or someone called for attention. It was vivid and loud, demanding her focus. There was much at stake. Fingers around the neck and squeezing symbolized a woman's voice cut off, a woman not permitted to be a woman.

Loneliness bore down on Eve like a millstone around a drowning person's neck. She arrived at the banks of the river. She wondered how it would be to float down the shimmering waters, facedown, arms spread wide. She wondered how it would be to swallow the last gulps of water.

Hypnotically, the water lulled her senses as she watched the ebb and flow. Dizziness made her sway. The pull into the water called as sirens offering solace and bliss. She touched a nearby tree branch and held tight. To let go would be easy, slipping in, drifting.

Images of Graciéla floated through her consciousness. Dizziness distracted her and further dimmed her mind. She tightened her grip on the branch. Shame bore down, her shoulders and head slumped. She needed to let go, to yield. The waters called. Bad love from bad men took and did not give. She hated her father. She hated herself. She could not dismiss the dark yearning. It had always been there. To no longer try had always been there.

Graciéla's presence faded. Quiet overtook her mind. She let go of the branch and walked on. A quiet rhythm of one foot in front of the other centered her energies. Despair had passed. The spirit of Graciéla exorcised evil.

Sometimes, Eve felt best when alone. It was familiar. Her mother had been alone. As a child, Eve had promised herself that it would not be so with her. She would have love. She would not be alone. And yet, here she was. Graciéla would listen to her when she spoke of such things. She would smile. She would say nothing. Eve remembered the old woman and did not feel alone.

She stopped walking, thin gray clouds floating overhead, the humid air wrapping comforting arms around her bare skin. The river was here. The river moved by. The river lapped to the banks near her feet, touching the tips of her leather shoes. Crusts of hardened mud cracked away from the banks where she stood. She watched clods and clumps of dried mud break off and float away.

Her father, a man of shadows, floated into the night, away from the little girl who lived along the river. The water pooled around her feet. She had stepped too close the edge. There was quicksand there, she could tell. Underground water pooled up to clay and silt. Sand particles floated within the dense water. Light from the full moon glistened along pinpricks of black glass-like stone that undulated atop the quicksand.

A great white-horned owl hooted and resounded into the night. Eve looked but could not see the bird. *Memories of childhood do not die. They echo on*. Graciéla's presence remained a constant companion.

Muddy waters lapped over the sand embankments. Eve's shoes were wet, ankles as well. Water curved around mud-baked corners. Quicksand and river water, Eve yielded her *triste*, sadness and memories and the cries of the little girl fading into the night.

Eve walked back through the forest. Gabriél waited patiently beside the taxi, bluish moonlight emanating as an aura from her friend and guardian of the night.

CHAPTER 9

G abriél waved as he drove away from Eve's home, disappearing into the night like a spirit. There one moment, and then gone.

Eve entered her comfortable university-area adobe and went to her backyard garden. The night air was dry with wisps of humidity rising from the earth. Abundant autumn produce and rich soil were a balm for a restless mind.

It was two a.m. Cicadas had long ceased chirping. Fragrances of vegetation and wet earth breathed sweetly. The full moon lingered in the jet-black sky of Aztlan del Sur. The deity hovered, Tonatzé, Goddess of the wild and free.

Eve reached down into the rich garden soil. Memories surfaced of the earth she touched at her mother's funeral, the pine box laid into the ground on a windy, winter night. Eve tossed clumps of rich soil atop the coffin and said goodbye to her mother. On the outside, she had said goodbye. On the inside, fate scratched and clawed deep.

Other widows wept at the graveside. There were no men. These were the women of no men. They stood by one another

and wept. She had become her mother. Her mother's breath moved through her throat and lungs, rasping. She gasped and bent over, her forehead touching the ground.

Her mother, a woman with long, raven-black hair and bronze skin, appeared. As a hologram flickering in the garden, her mother grazed her neck with a cold and damp palm. Her mother cradled the top of her head. Eve could not move. Fate grabbed the back of her skull. The pressure became painful. Eve doubled over tight, head to core trembling.

The backyard became translucent. Moonlight grew bright. Her mother vanished under the gaze of the night moon. The moon hovered as a Goddess, Tonatzé, azure and lustrous. There was only blue light now and garden and a woman shaken, lying on the earth, drifting to sleep.

Eve awakened, cradled in her garden by warm earth, a bluish nighttime glow illuminating the sprawling garden vegetation, dozens of orange and white pumpkins and streamers, abundant tomatillos wrapped in sheer casings, squash, lettuce, cucumbers, and chiles a vibrant crimson.

The night was a hallowed quiet. Breaths drew soft and easy. Her thoughts lit on Sam. With his friends, misogyny surged. He morphed into a man who demanded and got. He craved bronze skin. They all did. White guys set on lording it over bronze women. It's what they did and how they thought, how they demanded and how they got. Eve knew the type.

Her hands shook, and she dug into the moist earth of her well-tended garden, the fertile soil soothing to strong hands. Terrible winds kicked up, and lightning cracked along the nighttime horizon-to-horizon panorama of Aztlan del Sur. Electrical currents whipped through high-desert air as the timing of thunder and lightning told of storms over the Jemez Mountains making their way to the city. Atmospheric electricity stood the ends of Eve's arm hairs on end, strands of her shoulder-length, auburn hair floating eerily.

Winds intensified and slender ash trees bent. Thin branches snapped. A foul odor of rotten eggs came and went. Eve's hair whipped wildly across her face then flew out to the sides as if to spark and catch fire.

She kneaded the dark and wet soil. Lightning ceased, and her hair floated to her shoulders. An owl hooted in the thirty-foot elm whose branches spread across half the backyard. The old owl was the keeper of secrets.

The farthermost northern edge of her garden drew Eve's gaze. No one walked there. During parties and departmental events, people overlooked the quiet corner. Darkness tucked into its sleeve what lay in plain sight. Even the sacred coven of friends kept their distance from the lone earth space. Unknown to anyone, Eve buried there the remnants of man encounters. Combs, snapshots, gifts. She kept it secret, for to speak of it was to weaken the magic.

A gray-brown, green-eyed owl hooted. It fed on rodents, insects, and small birds. It was a sit-and-wait predator. Local lore considered the owl a shape-shifter's spirit animal. When the green-eyed owl propitiously arrived, Eve's friends and associates were startled. She never commented.

Once, an inebriated male professor had become sexually insistent with Eve. Others had cleared out after a year-end party, backyard deserted. He cornered Eve against the wall, arms stretched out on either side, pinning her against the gray block.

Rattler quick, the owl targeted and attacked. Claws scraped against the pink scalp of the six-foot-two Anglo. Hoot, hoot, hoots sounded like the firing of wartime guns. The pedant professor fell backward, eyes wide as saucers, scholarly mind petrified, black chunky glasses cracked on sandstone boulders.

Monday morning at the university had drawn applause Eve's way from female faculty. Word had spread. Dejected cock hoped to taint the reputation of one deemed hard to get and harder to bed. He whispered of frigid female academics. She taunted then teased but didn't thaw, he jested. It was tittle-tattle to gossip about craven fools, spoken by one with white tape fastening the corners of his thick, black plastic glasses.

Señor professor's contusions never completely healed. Gashes and scratches spontaneously bled whenever he mentioned Eve's name. At midterm, he hastily departed for another university position, some said under the cover of night.

Shoveled into the soil, a foot down, lay his monogrammed handkerchief and wallet photo of himself.

Then there was the landscape architect. He came to *lend a hand*. He and Eve had met at a local garden center, one conversation leading to another. He offered his expertise, Eve accepting.

Eve had to give him credit. It wasn't until the day's work was done—concrete poured, bricks laid, and manure spread—that the architect morphed and slithered. He was a weapon seeking discharge.

The owl descended, left the architect clawed and scratched. Under the loamy black soil lay his leather gloves and stubby pencil, testaments to foiled plans and an abrupt ending. Professor and architect got off easy.

The owl was fierce and potentially deadly.

CHAPTER 10

A t three a.m., the proverbial witching hour of Aztlan, Sweet Mary left her apartment for the gathering of Las Brujas Malas, deep in the crumbling limestone edifice of vicious spirits. The condemned downtown limestone church, once a prosperous enclave of the Ecclesia Dei, had long been abandoned. It sat adjacent to Sweet Mary's bedroom, badly stained by gray and black soot. Putrid odors of the cursed underworld that lay beneath its unhallowed edifice, curled through the atmosphere surrounding the decaying structure.

Sweet Mary wound her way past the fenced and barbed wired blockade that deterred homeless souls and nighttime vandals. Her lithe frame smoothly squeezed between the slightly ajar, chained doors. She walked over the toppled wooden pews and stone statues littering the concrete flooring from the back of the church to its altar. The religious artifacts had been defaced by those news media referred to as sledgehammer-wielding lunatics claiming clerical abuse as children.

She quipped to herself, *Religion mocks, uses, and abuses. Nothing new under the black sun.*

She opened a narrow side door that led to a rusted iron spiral staircase. Into the haunted and torch-lined basement that stretched thirty feet beneath the surface, she stepped. At the final stair, she touched bare earth. Torches were lit along a cave of mirrors, shards embedded in the walls, shattered remnants taken from the homes of victims who had defamed Las Brujas.

Anyone who dared speak ill of the brujas ended the day tormented, injured, or maimed. Crises happened. One second they were safe, the next mowed down by an out-of-control car, or mugged and cut, or worse, lured in by a soft and sexy vixen loaded with a nasty biological curse. Mirrors confiscated from homes during nighttime raids reflected the victim's horrified face when doom struck.

Sweet Mary hurried past the legions of rats scampering away from her every step into the cracks and crevices of the century-old limestone structure. An unavoidable eyesore at the heart of one the most decayed areas of the often-sinister downtown Aztlan del Sur. It was a meeting place of a multiplicity of worlds, where street and abyss had grimy corridors littered with violent souls and heart-wrenching cries of the desperate and doomed.

In this haunted zone, Sweet Mary presided over the witches of black magic. They knew how to spot love, taint love, kill love. It's what bad mothers did. It's what Las Brujas did. It's what Sweet Mary did—because what had been received must be given.

No one knew where they gathered. Evil demanded hiddenness. Street-smart folk and fear-ridden church folk knew them as Las Brujas Malas, the foulest of witches, not to be crossed. Even those who suspected the whereabouts of their lair dared not cross the street to look at the unholy building, now a crumbling religious edifice.

The witches met at the mouth of a deserted tunnel, which in former years led to the secret chapel of the reigning archbishop, who there entertained a bevy of female devotees. Las Brujas, the four desert urban witches, walked down the twenty-foot descent. Hard-pack dirt sloped gently into the entrance of the unhallowed region of the chapel that had become the accursed cave of Las Brujas. They moved forward, into the mouth of the cave. It lay deep in the bowels of the basement, a forty-by-forty-foot area.

Torches, posted every six feet along the reinforced walls, cast eerie shadows that danced and pointed accusatory fingers reflected in the warbled shards of mirror. They appeared then disappeared randomly. Las Brujas knew each shift signaled another soul snuffed out and jettisoned into the bowels of this blasphemous realm. The air breathed cold and harsh. Moisture from exhalations hung in the atmosphere like sharpened black fingernails. They glistened then faded. The air was frigid.

Sweet Mary was the first to reach the ritual area and waited at the center. It was an encirclement of limestone and granite. She removed the soiled figurine of Miché from beneath her flowing cloak. Piles of cedar branches lay against interior limestone and granite walls. Red, iron-rich earth served as flooring. At the center of the hallowed realm lay large, crisscrossed cedar logs that had been ablaze for decades, flames never dying out.

Sharp crackles of cedar echoed through the underground chamber. Shadows cast from the glow of flickering fires danced across the walls, netherworld spirits caught in a silent reverie of dance. Smoke did not rise. It curled into the ground, called to do so by ancient layers of inner earth where gods old and foul resided.

The four did not speak. Glances, nods, and silence were exchanged. Tales of things dark and dastardly passed wordlessly between them. They gathered around the fire. Sweet Mary, dressed in layers of colorful *pueblo* wraps, swept her left hand over the darkness. In her right hand, she delicately held the corrupted Goddess. There appeared, out of a dimension beyond normal reckoning, a four-foot-long log.

Dark forces rippled like visible currents of air from the circle of the four. Psychic waves swelled then receded like tumultuous ocean currents. An intimate connection bound each woman to a kingdom of terrible energies, nature run amok.

Sweet Mary bowed her head to the fire. She lowered herself to the log. Placing the statuette of Michté on the ground before her, she adjusted her seated position and raised her head as the presider over Las Brujas Malas. According to legend, the log served as a throne for other presiders from decades and centuries past, the figurine accompanying each one, age after evil age.

But Sweet Mary knew the perverse truth. She was the one and only who had survived beyond the normal lot of seventy years accorded to Las Brujas of Aztlan. For more than five centuries, she had presided over gatherings of brujas. The arrival of the Cross-and-Crown of Spain had ushered in terrifying spirits. With each generation of brujas, Sweet Mary's lethal nature swelled.

La Michté, Goddess of ruination and decay, grew deadlier.

The three others made their way to their respective places

on smaller logs before the roaring fire. Out of respect, the younger two waited for the oldest bruja, Geralda with her hip-length white hair floating around her shoulders, to lower her elfin self onto a flattened rock. Even though the most aged, Geralda's wicked magic exerted a violence seen in women half her age. With hardly a furrow on her brow, her powers burned white hot. A flick of her right index finger and boulders exploded, leaving nothing but a neat little cone-shaped pile of dust. What she could do to flesh and blood was beyond description, a man or woman would be present one second and the next disintegrated.

The third bruja, Orlinda, always dressed in black cashmere. She painted her fingernails black as her raven hair, smooth as silk and said to reflect the image of her latest victim. She lowered herself to the flooring with the grace and ease of a gazelle.

Lastly, Hortensia, swathed in her customary red silk, sat so lightly on her log that a fly wouldn't have been disturbed. Her fame lay in her ability to curse by casting a gaze and sucking through barely parted lips the vitality of a soul taken in as juice through a straw. Victims stood wide-eyed, paralyzed, and then fainted. They remained comatose for days, then awoke remembering nothing save the eerie sounds of wraith-like inhalations.

Raging and the taking of energy bonded the four brujas. They knew the rage of no love—the fathers who were no fathers and the religion of the fathers—Ecclesia Dei that took love and killed love.

La Michté, mirror shards, gleaming tungsten knife, and sealed packets of fresh blood were lined up on the hard-pack earth, black magic implements, tools of a vile trade. Smoke, fine curls of cedar, spiraled upward then speedily downward from the center of the flames, an unseen force sucking vapors down. A barely perceptible hum rattled the sandstone and granite walls. Bits of sand crumbled from the roof and floated onto the skin of the entranced women.

Atoms, molecules, light waves crackled. Pungent whiffs of sulphur emanated from the center of the cavern. Mirror shards reflected the light of the fires. Eyes closing, the four entered a realm of trance and spells. They entered a visionary world of writhing snakes and surreal webs spun by coal-black spiders.

Sounds of women screaming and dying raked across nerve endings. Legions of ghostly crones drifted out of blackened walls, specters of centuries past. Las Brujas Malas wore no clothing, apparel shed in the ghostly transition from underworld to netherworld.

Sparks of light, like red fireflies, rippled through the rank atmosphere and danced over the skin of Las Brujas. Odors of decay, human waste, and mineral deposits from the earth's center polluted the atmosphere.

A numinous orb pulsed out of the distance. It came from the gloomiest recess of the cave. Casting a sinister glow, it penetrated the eye as splinters of obsidian. Spires of sandstone jettisoned out of the earth and encircled the orb that hovered above the fire. The howling of forsaken women echoed through the netherworld.

Sweet Mary turned a rage-ridden face toward the others. Where her eyes should have been were sockets, worms oozing out of the serrated black holes. The sockets became tainted mirrors, and she wailed. Las Brujas wailed a requiem of loss and eternal grief.

Communication leaped from mind to mind. Visions ran quick across the mirrors lodged in Sweet Mary's eyes, images of blood flowing into the Rio Grande River. Adult-sized bodies bobbed up and down like dislodged buoys—a man, obese and drowned by the ingestion of water and blood.

The other was a woman, her face betraying tormented years; her body picked up and tossed into bubbling mounds of wet earth bordering the river. Undulating earth sucked her under, into a hungry maw of earth. On the far side of the river, three women watched horrified. Eyes that were also sockets became mirrors shattered.

CHAPTER 11

S weet Mary opened her eyes, refreshed from a night of tormented sleep. Nightmares cleared her mind. She stretched long and deep in bed, the imprint of her body carved into the stained mattress after years of motionless sleeping.

Nightly terrors held her in a paralyzed state. She was aware of dreaming. During the nightmare, she had tried to cry out and open her eyes but could not. No matter the effort, there was no sound and no escape for Sweet Mary.

Doctors diagnosed chronic, severe bipolar disorder with psychosis. Some said there were multiple personalities, the result of a childhood trauma. Three other personalities had been identified, each more envious than the other, hate targeted on the good.

Drugs aplenty had been prescribed. Sweet Mary led the pill doctors to believe she'd taken the mind-numbing concoctions and was stable. Egos swelled. They'd done what practitioners before considered impossible. Pill doctors signed her off as dischargeable, no longer in need of forced hospitalization.

In and out of psychiatric hospitals throughout her teenage years—before she learned to work the system—she suffered terribly and inflicted terrible things in terrible ways. Hospitalists were not conversant with the heritage and wiles of Sweet Mary. Windows spontaneously shattering, electrical blackouts throughout the hospital, locked wards of paranoid schizophrenics simultaneously breaking loose with nerve-shredding screams when she lost her temper. Finally, they tied it to her. They witnessed how her temper affected objects, minds, and mirrors.

If patients, staff, doctors, and visitors gazed even for a moment into a nearby mirror when in her presence, the glass cracked, slowly, loudly, scarily. No one caught on at first that the display had to do with Sweet Mary. Then a high-ranking hospital administrator witnessed a Sweet Mary supernatural event and told a shocked audience that the horror never happened unless she was present, watching, scoffing.

A highly regarded behavioral neuroscientist spoke before his grand rounds at the hospital. He admitted there was no evidence that Sweet Mary somehow cracked the mirrors from afar. However, the scientist did correlate the string of nightmarish happenings in the hospital to her appearance. "There is no causal proof here," he noted then added, "Tests have proven, however, that the patient's disturbed electromagnetic field issues from a chronically psychotic psyche."

Peering over his glasses, he punctuated his remarks to esteemed colleagues by saying, "This is an example of C.G. Jung's research on synchronicity. The inner world causes changes in the outer world. Disturbance within makes for disturbance without. Mary is the most disturbed patient we have ever treated."

Hospital staff eagerly expedited Sweet Mary's discharge. It was simple enough once she acted stable. She looked stable, played stable, gave them what they wanted, and she got what she wanted. Discharged.

Black drapes with thick black vinyl liners kept the early morning sunlight from Sweet Mary's apartment bedroom. Sunlight tormented the black divinity cradled within her breast. It was a savage and hungry force.

She stretched and remembered her dreams, her luscious nightmares. In a granite and limestone cave of shadows gathered what doctors called the multiples: Geralda, Orlinda, and Hortensia.

Even as a child, dreams had become nightmares. Physicians and psychotherapists were caught in the spell of her stories and dreams. She loved it. She lured them into her web and swallowed their horrified expressions, their terror. Their souls.

They left therapy sessions stunned, gabbing nervously to themselves, stroking their arms and shoulders as if to ward away malignant energy. Sweet Mary stored their energy, let it bubble and boil, and then used it against them. One after another, they witnessed their lives turn catastrophic. Marriages ended. Finances turned south. Lives drained away by self-inflicted slashing of carotid arteries.

While in the asylum, Sweet Mary suffered memories, gruesome and lingering. The nuns in the orphanage had burned her with their clothes pressing iron, buttocks and back scalded. *You pay for sins, little Mary. Little Mary, poor little Mary.* They scoffed. They scoffed for a while, then scoffed no more. The nuns fueled her fury.

Las Brujas saved a little girl, came to her when she needed

them most. In nightmares, they told her of ritual acts—victims dragged into a mirrored cave and spread eagle, a shining black obsidian knife, slitting throat to genitals as they watched themselves writhe along the mirrored walls of the cave of Las Brujas Malas.

Preternatural darkness lingered in Sweet Mary's bedroom. It kept Las Brujas close, witch energy thriving in lightlessness, the shadowy depth of bewitched musing and utter despair.

Without darkness, her mind threatened to fracture. Into a million pieces, it would disintegrate. She could see it; she could feel it, the ever-present threat of total disintegration. Flying apart into a million psychic pieces did not do a witch's mind good.

Sunlight was simply unpleasant. It yanked her from the womb as a fetus bobbing in cold bathtub water. Memories inscribed themselves into the body as well as the mind, and she trembled, muscles tightening, tendons and bones aching. She rubbed her legs and arms, face and neck, until her skin heated and relief set in.

As a woman, she suffered for days and nights after exposure to the light of the sun. Headaches, migraines, throbbing lights, voices, voices of men, fingers, hands, and bodies writhing, terrible things being done. She'd suffered in the light, so in the dark, her domain, she was the one who inflicted suffering. It was pleasant.

She smiled and stretched out like a black alley cat on crumbling brick wall. Lingering in bed, she inhaled the haunting smell of sulphur that lingered after her nightly sojourns.

Images of Sam Shear, *the man who can because I love him so*, brought swells of desire. Underworld excursions engorged passion. Many a time they lay together but not as man and woman. Sam the Man nestled into Sweet Mary as a child to a mother. He spoke of matters trivial to her yet to him, weighty and worrisome. She eased his mind, then inserted herself into his mental nether regions. Instructions were given mind-to-mind; warnings seared into gray convolutions of the brain. He was hers. Sam the Man was soldered to Sweet Mary. Women came and went, no challenge to her.

Until now.

Turning on her stomach, she reached between her thighs. Unutterable sensations seeped into crevices and folds. Quivers started through mind and flesh. Her lips curled upward. Sam had committed himself to her, sworn the oath. Trembling in the downtown alley over a decade ago, a limp and withering man and a down-and-out lawyer, he knelt and kissed her outstretched hand as he uttered the words,

Never to seek another love.
Never to find another love.
Never to have another love.

He had Sweet Mama Mary's love. She gave a final squeeze between her thighs and screamed.

Minutes later, Sweet Mary stood naked and went to the foot of her rusted iron bed. A mound of earth scraped from her mother's grave appeared each morning, three feet in diameter, cradling the instruments of her craft. The statuette of Michté, a gleaming tungsten blade, shards of mirror, and a sealed bag of blood were set in the center of the mix of clay, sand, and limestone. Each morning, they appeared then vanished at the completion of the ritual.

She knelt before the mound and touched the oily resin

head of the figurine. It became spirit. Mother Michté ascended from earthen mound to sky, the apartment ceiling yielding to the ascent.

The sack of blood spontaneously ripped open and blanketed the mound in crimson red, and the tungsten knife stood at attention. The shard reflected the dark elegance of the Queen of Death.

Michté made her way upward and disappeared.

Sweet Mary rose from her knees. The mound had vanished, implements gone. Magic infused her. She looked at the faded and torn poster tacked to the wall in front of her bed, carcasses of animals and birds hanging upside down from trees along the bosque in Aztlan del Sur, a blood-hungry hunt finalized and celebrated.

Electricity surged through her core. The time drew nigh. Never did prey escape her talons.

Naked, she opened the front door. Frigid autumnal winds whipped out of alleyways. A rat the size of a small cat rolled across her bare feet. She laughed.

The morning newspaper, the *Aztlan Crier*, lay at her doorstep. She remained sheltered under the apartment's awning from direct sunlight. The morning light touching her skin hurt, made sizzling sounds like gristle on a frying pan. Blisters rose from her skin then receded when she withdrew to the shadows. She had instructed the paperboy to place the *Crier* under the eaves, the terrified youngster immediately obedient. Reaching for the paper, she caught the unsurprising but pleasing headlines. Front-page pictures could be gruesome. She smiled.

He was as bloated as the dream portended. Images of the blubbery judge bobbing up and down along the Rio Grande River made Sweet Mary wonder what the professional community would think of their esteemed, elected official. Once a year, Sweet Mary landed a well-regarded community member onto the front page of the local tabloid. Men who kept secret company with the erotic black witch of downtown Aztlan del Sur got the message.

Couples living in swanky condominiums a block away walked home, hand in hand in front of her. They were out for a lovely morning walk. They gawked at the naked Sweet Mary, stopping and whispering in one another's ears.

Sweet Mary pretended not to notice, and then to be embarrassed before she looked and smiled, her visage supernaturally shifting to a mouthful of rotten teeth on a pustule-riddled face of an ancient hag spewing curses.

The couple blanched, sweeping their hands to their mouths, horrified, and ran around the corner of the block quicker than the rat that chased and nibbled at their heels. A woman's midmorning screams and a man's wimpy shrieks, nothing short of delicious. First-of-the morning mischief very nearly beat a cup of savory Colombian Joe proffered by Sweet Mary's favorite coffee shop, *Hellendo*. She loved playing quick and dirty tricks. Pretentious downtown urbanites were easy pickings, unsuspecting dupes.

The image of a soon-to-be second corpse floating atop the waters of the old river pressed to mind. This one would also be featured in the *Aztlan Crier*, front-page gossip. Shivers quickened her pulse. One so naïve needed to be ended. The lure was set.

Another surprise lay in the offing.

During the night, Sweet Mary had spotted the celestial protector. From miles away, one known as Gabriél had witnessed her terrifying display on the West Mesa. She appeared as a huge, spinning tumbleweed, ablaze with a blackened center radiating red and white-tipped flames. The wheel of fire burst into energy that scorched the earth.

He'd been warned.

Sweet Mary brooked no challengers. She ended betrayers, contenders, and protectors alike. There was no escape from the long arm of Sweet Mary, Queen of Death.

CHAPTER 12

The four women entered the hallowed yoga area of the metaphysical bookstore, a pine floored, twelve by fifteen foot light blue, dimly lit room. It was midmorning, their weekly Saturday time to practice the ancient postures, *asanas*, and meditation. It gave them an infusion of spiritual strength when most needed.

Eve had already prepared the room. At the front of the space was a low-lying antique Indonesian ironwood table Graciéla had garnered from a downtown flea market. Atop it rested a brass depiction of a dancing Shiva, the yogi's source of inspiration. Along with the symbol of Shiva were four red candles, stones of obsidian, quartz, lapis, and turquoise. Fresh and colorful Aztlan wildflowers graced the area on the floor directly beneath the table.

Shirley, Samantha, and Tanya, dressed in loose fitting cotton clothing, placed their earth-toned mats in a semi-circle around the table. They seated themselves in lotus position, legs crossed, and feet on opposing thighs.

The one window at the east side of the room, covered by

white sheers, allowed in filtered rays of Aztlan sunshine.

Eve sounded the yogic mantra "OM," each of them joining their voices. The sound faded, each voice ending slightly later than the one before it. Eve's voice finished last.

They rose to their feet at the head of their mats and began a silent sequencing of flowing postures. Diaphragmatic nostril breathing, backbends, forward folds, head to knee movements, and side stretches were gracefully executed, held, and repeated.

Minutes passed, now nearing an hour, and the four moved to a seated position to begin floor sequencing. From cobra pose, half locust, rabbit and camel, and spinal twists they moved through the age-old rite. Their breaths were resonant and sounded gently from their diagram as ocean waves lapping against the shore.

An hour and a half later, after completing the yogic headstand, they sat once again in lotus position. Eyes shut, they concentrated at brow point.

Shirley intoned the final rounds of the mantra, "OM," after which they laid back on their mats for the last resting posture, *savasana*.

Energy coursed from the top of their heads to the soles of their feet.

After three or four minutes, they turned to the side, rose to their feet, rolled up their mats, and silently left the yogic practice area.

After yoga, the morning was crammed with things to do, each one flipping through Eve's mind like West Mesa tumbleweeds on a stormy day. She looked forward to Saturdays. There was yoga. This intimate communion with friends, a time of inner nourishment. Then there were home chores, errands, and meandering. Saturdays were packed with things to do, places to go, people to see, and unforeseen happenings.

She'd put on jogging gear. Later in the morning, she'd run. First, there were chores to whip through. She deemed herself an Aztlan tornado when it came to completing weekly household tasks.

In less than three hours, especially after the energy infusion from yoga, Eve made breakfast and whisked through the cleaning of her three-bedroom adobe home. She went on to a handful of errands: grocery store, post office, and dry cleaners. She'd gone from activity to activity like lightning tearing up the sky.

Her energy could be hypomanic, a psychologist friend said. "Need to watch it," he said. "Or it'll spin out and take you down. Use too much energy, and it takes a bad toll, takes you down and out because everything's been used up, nothing left inside to replenish. Always need to leave a little inside because it'll grow more," he said.

Today, she risked it. There was a pressing need to figure out what was scratching in her soul like rats on wallboard. When she hit this mental zone, energy had to be focused, even when it came to love. She hazarded hitting a dismal bottom with spiked limestone walls. It's how she remembered the man ordeal of months ago, and this one could be nasty. But there had to be risk if there was a chance of gain.

Chores done, errands completed, she retied her running shoes, clicked the front door shut, and dead bolted it. Nearly out of breath with a tension headache in the offing, she stretched and took off at a steady pace.

Headaches normally stopped once exercise endorphins pumped through her blood vessels and her heart pounded. Her breaths grew graceful and rhythmic. But her heart beat unevenly, breaths pulled jagged and shallow. Pressure built. Primal forces called. She needed the wilds of nature. Then she'd catch her pace and steady her heart, her breath would recover a natural flow.

The bosque beckoned, the forest of Aztlan del Sur, largest of its kind in North America.

Bosque had called since the first of the day, lit up along the white screen of mind. The white screen of mind proffered psychic messages. Words and images appeared and lingered. She had to get there, to the lonesome forest with its whispering breezes and river tides of memories and things to come.

What's worth loving is worth fighting for. Graciéla's mental impression took hold of her fractious mind, her words about love unexpected were unsettling. Eve didn't want to think anymore about love, to go there in her mind, to so much as yield for an instant to the possibility that she was falling into its grasp. She shook her head as though by doing so, she could ward off vulnerability.

She kept her run at a rapid clip. *Beware. There are traps, mindtraps. Old ghosts and new demons. Nature will help. It exorcises fears.* The old one continued, *Wild nature—wild woman. Wild nature—wild woman.*

Spontaneously, Eve intoned the words of the incantation sung by the four women of life, nature, and the way of all things, the wild women of Aztlan,

She is lone and she is wild
She is Goddess of the Wild Thing

She is near
She is near…

Her heart suddenly welled with missing and loss for a true friend, one now closer in death than in life.

She is near
She is near…

Graciéla was near, far off yet close. Eve wondered about death. An academic and scholar of ancient texts, she remained a neophyte in the mysteries of love, life, and death.

Forty minutes later, by her digital watch, she arrived at the dirt path marking the entrance to the preserved forest. Her mind whirled with energy. She walked down the dirt path that led to the Rio Grande. There was an uneasy sense in the atmosphere. An eerie silence descended. Morning sparrows ceased their song abruptly, as Eve entered the hallowed bosque of Aztlan del Sur.

Sparrows darted from trees and flew overhead. At first, their wings were frantic, flapping roughly out of rhythm. Then they rose to a higher air current and circled, calm and purposefully.

Eve recognized the ritualistic movement. It was a shamanic warding, bird apparition of shaman shape-changers. They protected their own. Guardian spirits appeared out of unseen worlds into the realm of the everyday.

Eve's college courses thoroughly investigated the paranormal, shamanic activity integral to Aztlan lore and magic. Unwanted, outside influences could be blocked, old mystic texts taught. The Sandia Mountains rose a mile high to the east, Rio Grande river rippling alongside to the west, turquoise-blue sky above, crisp autumn leaves and high-desert sand below. Protective elements of earth, air, sky, water, and ether encircled Eve.

Ether conjured shielding spirits. Mystics of old taught of the protective value of elemental magic. Natural magical energies, intuited by wise souls, were real as subtle desert breezes.

Energy change signals a spiritual shift. Listen and take to heart. Graciéla's words lingered. *Goddess is close.*

Brown sparrows circled overhead seven times and then flew south. Despite the omen, Eve's skin crawled. A chill pierced her to the bone. She shuddered. She walked along the dusty forest path. Danger sparked with each movement of a branch or twig. The narrow path was considered safe. River with random kayakers on one side, a bike path on the other, she wasn't secluded. There were usually late morning walkers out. Today, Eve was alone.

She should leave. She could pack a brisk pace home. But she knew if fears weren't faced, they'd return. When they came back, they were burlier, more vicious. She didn't want that, the horror of truth twisted into a nightmare. It could happen as easy as running quickly from an unrelenting specter only to discover a more gruesome ghost at every fork in the road.

Anxiety staved off, Eve persisted along the dusty trail. The silence was deafening. A wild thumping of her heart sounded loudly in her ears. She couldn't make sense of her body's warnings. She felt sharp, alert, and ready for anything.

After fifteen minutes, she arrived at the banks of the Rio Grande, waters making their way choppily down the curving embankments to Mexico.

Heartbeats picked up an already rapid clip. Palms were sweaty. Her body was tighter than a taut rubber band about ready to snap. Muscles and tendons throbbed. Dull then sharp pains demanded attention, a message from a truthful body to a sometimes slow-on-the-emotional-uptake mind. Clenching her teeth, she caught her breath and gazed at the water's edge. She wanted to see, to pick up on what was trying to save her stubborn ass from unnecessary woes.

Muddy edges appeared to crawl with snakes. But rattlers didn't inhabit this zone, and water snakes didn't contort and gyrate weirdly. Her jaws clenched and muscles tightened so severely a jagged pain ripped up her left side to her temples, pulsations hot, and sweat trickling down her cheek. She wiped away the perspiration and watched the odd twisting of normally organic shapes and movements.

Earth undulated and opened like little mouths looking to feed. She pulled back, fright kicking up further as when she once spotted a swarm of wasps on the attack, her hands clenching, brain stunned. She was held in place by either obstinacy or courage.

The compulsion to hightail it out of the haunted landscape kicked up higher. She stifled it. She could shove down and kill feelings good and bad. She was masterful and wished the mastery would one day go one way or the other. Wobbling on a psychic fence of right and wrong did nothing but land a person ass down, spine twisted, and stunned. It was never good. She braced herself, drew breaths deep and long, and rubbed her eyes. The earth no longer twisted and twirled.

The next second her knees buckled, and she went down. Ground sucked her in, gave way as though she'd been standing on mud, camouflaged somehow by distractions and shifting desert light. Gurgling earth grabbed and pulled her ankles and calves with hundreds of little fingers. She sank into a gurgling earth.

Quicksand.

Immediately, she quashed panic, didn't let it take her fully into its hungry grasp. If she didn't struggle, she'd sink only to her waist or armpits. Weight displaced the mix of sand and water. Descent ceased. She'd float if she didn't cave to terror.

Quicksand didn't swallow calm people. It swallowed the anxiety stricken; death sure as sunset on an open mesa at day's end. Steadied nerves were best. She locked her mind on survival.

Suction was strong. Uneasy tightness gripped her ankles and thighs. This was not supposed to happen; things were to ease as she eased. The fingers of wet earth did not ease. She stayed still. Squirming would be dangerous.

Bubbles formed atop the grayish-brown surface and popped like someone from below playing with mud and with a woman's soon-to-snap mind. If she didn't know better, she'd swear someone was watching and breathing from below the surface.

A face appeared in her mind's eye. It was as though she looked at a mirror that told of things unseen to the common eye. She saw the scowl of a witch. Eve winced. The witch was familiar and horrid. She'd seen her in the glass that night at the cantina. Eve stayed with the dreadful vision, didn't shift her gaze. Everything in her wanted to scream. The witch's eyes were filled with envy, hate malicious and lethal.

The vision lingered then vanished. Bubbles ceased. Evil energy remained and bile flooded her mouth. At her last physical, Eve's doctor had warned of a possible peptic ulcer. Eve knew it was from chronic stress. Bile reflux hit hard during intense stress. She gagged then spit and spit again. Vomit followed. Greenish-yellow fluid disappeared into the mud.

She was careful not to move her core. Yoga practice had strengthened her central muscles and diaphragm. She willed her body to remain as stiff as possible even while gagging and vomiting.

It worked. She didn't go down any farther; she no longer felt the nausea. She no longer needed to vomit.

Bubbles began again, this time enlarged and violently popping. Sprays of mud whipped across Eve's cheeks, stung enough that she wondered if bits of sand had penetrated her skin and drawn blood. She closed then opened her eyes. Mud dripped down her field of vision, but she didn't dare to try to move her hands out of the muddy mess. Wipe away mud drips and there'd be an immediate end to a bad situation.

Her stomach had emptied. Bad taste stayed. Head swam with vestiges of nausea and haunting images of a witch's stare.

A local tale of an old woman, a witch, *La Llorona*, washed across her blurry mind. The woman, embittered from love going bad, drowned her children in a fit of anger. Other renditions of the story said that La Llorona was known by many names, one of them Michté, a woman barren due to a mother's failed abortion. It damaged internal organs and left mind states beyond repair, rendered an adult woman infertile through no fault of her own. An absence of a love life drove a desperate woman to strange and terrible acts. To this day, unsuspecting victims drowned inexplicably in the Rio Grande.

Allegedly, Rio Grande quicksand gurgled, came alive. Foul breaths of La Llorona, Michté, enlivened earth, sand, and mud. Victims were sucked into an underworld abyss of witches. Bodies returned to the overworld, bobbing and floating down current to Mexico.

Eve taught students that unresolved loss or unrequited love led many a woman to foul deeds. They lost heart—soul. They morphed into witches, entitled creatures. They seized what they wanted, how they wanted it. Eve lectured on tales of La Llorona, Michté, as archetype and symbol, metaphor of a love-spurned mother turned envious and devouring.

But here Eve was, paralyzed. Waves of gurgling and quicksand were no metaphor. Agitation could turn bad to worse. Eve clutched harder for a stable mind. It was a torment, nearly impossible not to panic. She gritted her teeth, tightened her mental hold. Gently, millimeter by millimeter, she managed to raise her right hand. Mud offered no resistance. She raised her right forearm out of the hungry maw of dirt and grit. She grabbed hold of a desert oak's dropping branch. It held firm. Five fingers clutched like a vise. She lifted her left arm and hand. Inch by inch, she loosened her torso from the deadly mud. Low-lying olive tree branches gave steadier purchase.

Relief.

Memories of circling sparrows, an ancient warding against fated demise, provided a moment's comfort. She pulled upward. Branches did not snap or break. They were supple. Evenly, she pulled with breath after concentrated breath. She gazed toward the sky. There were no sparrows overhead. The silence felt unnerving.

The sky shifted, turquoise bright turned to leaden gray. The desert olive branch snapped. Eve screamed and dropped.

She sank to her shoulders. Quicksand lapped up past her chin, grains of sand forming crusts along her lips. Clenching her teeth, she was grateful her mind hadn't snapped along with the branch. Wits kept panic at bay.

Dying wasn't a concern, survival was. It was the getting there that mattered—how it happened, how she did it. She detested the thought of dying by a witch's curse, slipping into an underworld of final breaths and mud-loaded lungs. If she went down into the belly of the abyss and the mouth of a soul-famished witch, she'd do it on her terms.

Middle finger out.

CHAPTER 13

A voice rang out. "Where are you?"

Eve snapped out of her reverie. Mud curled tighter around her fingers. She tried to lift her hand. Her hand trembled beneath the gurgling mire. It was stuck. Her chest constricted. She feared a yell would make things worse. Rage fomented. She gritted her teeth, did her best to draw in energy and breath then yelled, "At the river—quicksand! Hurry!" She held tight. It was good to yell. She needed to yell.

Fear dissipated like a swarm of insects fluttering from a fire. Silence. Seconds froze. She'd heard a voice, a man's. She knew she'd heard a voice. It was someone she knew. Her mind was moving fast and wide as a blast of buckshot. There was a man out there, he'd called out, but silence came and stayed. She knew he'd called out.

Mud squeezed tight then tighter. Her ribs ached. They could crack, splinter, and that pain was nothing she cared to dwell on. Mud did not cease its mounting pressure, millimeter by millimeter it squeezed.

Her mind spun, eyes closed, breathing nearly ceased.

Maybe there'd been no one there. Only a wish, an audible illusion. Things faded in and out, nearly to black. Black was good, she could go there and not come back. She'd always toyed with black.

A voice came again from the forest, resonant then up close. "Well, look at you. This is my place. I walk here to clear out my head. Didn't know you did too."

Vision cleared, mind ceasing its gut-churning dizziness. She knew him. It was annoying.

Sam was annoying, a fool. Anyone who uttered such trivia under these circumstances was a fool. He peered down at her and smiled. She did not answer the fool. She wanted him there. She wanted him gone. She was relieved. She was pissed. Rage was a friend, cleared her mind and set her resolve.

Sam smirked. He needed to go, to leave, back into the forest. That would be best, and then she would find a way out of the muck without the man who was a fool. She didn't trust him. Her mind space at the brow point opening flickered. Images of a paid private detective set on her trail. He'd been hired by Sam. Detective wired off text messages, Sam reacted quickly.

Sam stood there, watched, cocky. A mocking predator. Features morphed. Man changed. Eve looked into a funhouse mirror. Cocksure man attitude turned into empathic man. Sam's mind bent like branches in a windstorm. He blinked nervously. Something scratched at the insides of his head. He was a man at war.

Eve took the lead. "Gonna savor my demise or lend a hand?" Words came out pissed.

Sam didn't get it. He'd heard her. He'd blinked a couple of times in rapid succession when she spoke. His eyes were empty, presence fading to gone. But something lingered. The guy was in a mind fog. She knew that sensation. It'd passed only seconds ago. Sam shook his head hard, neck bones crackled. He muttered something unintelligible.

Crazy was real. Strain rolled across the big man's face. Neck muscles corded tight, carotid swelled. His head wobbled then straightened. He squinted then smiled. Sam was a kewpie doll.

Then he snapped loose. His countenance regained its human cast. Blood flushed through what had been gray and pasty. Eyes were now set hard. He nodded, "Sorry. Happens sometimes." He paused and reached deep inside. She could tell by the way he set his eyes harder and violently grit his jaws. "You'll owe me your life, I hope you know."

Fuck, fuck, fucker! Asshole can't stop himself. Eve's lips curled. Sam was totally full of shit. "Fuck you!" The mud gripped. She dropped down to her chin. "Fuck you, asshole!"

Sam watched, didn't move.

"Get the hell out of here." She sank to her lower lip. She didn't care. "I don't do debt." Her eyes burned a hole through the center of his forehead.

Son of a bitch turned and left, disappeared through forest brush.

Lungs squeezed against ribcage. Like a giant hand, the mud pressed in till her sides ached. It toyed with her, leaving a woman wondering as grit gurgled up and creased her lips. Breathing slowed to imperceptible yogic breaths. Old yogis could live for weeks buried underground. Slow nostril inhalations and maybe the sinking wouldn't happen too quickly.

She'd figure something out.

"Now don't go and give up." A long couple of minutes later, Sam's voice broke through the brush. His words were like ice chips shot into veins. They jolted her awake. She'd been losing consciousness, mud-creasing lips, nostrils barely sensing breath.

He held a red nylon rope, unbundled it, tied a lasso, and threw it around Eve's head. He nodded his head downward. The lasso smoothly slid down past her still visible nose then sunk down and under her chin. Again, he nodded, and the rope became taut.

Eve pressed chin to chest. The rope curled gently into her neck. It remained firm but not tight.

"Good. No payback. Freebie. Okay?"

She didn't say a thing. Man games didn't matter. She wanted out.

She tried to inch her head higher. It worked, and the rope contracted and inched farther downward. The mud gurgled violently. Her breath stopped, and she swallowed hard. Her eyes bulged. She looked at Sam. He held his gaze on the mud and didn't blink. Mud went down her throat. She coughed. The red rope pulled up. It wrapped itself around Eve's neck and yanked. She choked. Eve's head shot backward.

Sam shot out, "What the hell?" and stood wide-eyed.

The rope pulled again, this time upward but didn't tighten around Eve's neck. It pulled length from Sam's grasp. He gave it play like a line to a fishing rod. It flew vertically into the air, menacingly taut. It was a red cobra.

Sam didn't wince. His gaze shot downward, along the surface of the mud as if spotting something or someone below.

Straining to see, he stretched his head forward slightly. He cocked his right ear sideways as though to sharpen his hearing. He nodded and snapped out of some alternate state of mind. The rope went slack. He pulled the excess fiber his way.

The noose loosened. The mud gurgled and weirdly receded. It fell under Eve's shoulders and arms. She didn't so much as twitch. Sam held the rope firmly without tightening. Eve inched it further downward and made it snug under her arms. Once in place, Sam gave it a quick tug. Arm muscles bulging, he drew Eve up, quicksand loosening its clutch. Freed to the waist, she let Sam do the work. He pulled, strained, face reddened.

Eve didn't weigh much more than 120 pounds. Why a big-muscled, tall guy turned red-faced was anyone's guess. Suddenly, there was a yank from below. Then another tug. Eve was a plaything. The underworld force drew down aggressively. Sam pulled up. It yanked back violently.

There was a slap of the rope against the quicksand. Mud flew across Eve's eyes. Sam turned his head to the side and spit, outraged. He pulled and pulled hard. Seconds later, Eve was back on dry ground.

Sam sighed, wiped his brow, and sat on the ground beside her, clearly stunned. Eve pressed her palms to the earth. It was solid. She nearly cried with relief. She held back the tears, couldn't do tears, had done tears for too long.

She looked at Sam. Fixer-uppers were for real estate and not for men. She needed to bag this guy. He went back and forth more than a lunatic on amphetamines. Even though he'd saved her life, there'd be trouble. Read the signs and don't forget. Life-and-death helpful and down-deep torment weren't to be trusted.

A few seconds and she was on her feet, covered in mud from shoulder to toes, but safe and solid as a rock. She was pissed. She was grateful. She coughed up mud.

"You're welcome." Sam spoke with a nod of the head and steady, steel-blue eyes.

She looked at him and saw a cowering little boy beaten, bloody. His father stood over him with a blood-smeared back of the hand, mother fleeing out the back kitchen door, muttering compulsive little prayers to a plaster of Paris Jesus statue. She screamed like a crazy woman with her head on fire. This guy did crazy because he was raised with crazy. She didn't want in, had more than enough of her own.

Eve squeezed off the mud from her pants and shirt. "Well... thanks for the lift, Mr. Lawyer." She chuckled.

Sam did too. The guy was now sincere as could be. He was a bleating lamb along the Aztlan countryside.

Eve felt herself soften and hated it. It was the little boy coming through the harsh exterior of the man. She didn't want the softness. She didn't want to fall.

She smiled as she finished squeezing off the grime. "So, didn't want me to gurgle my way down? Didn't want homicide on your conscience?" Her words had an edge, glistening and sharp. So much for softness.

Sam lifted his eyebrows. "Well, as luck would have it, I had a rope in the trunk of my car." He paused then added, "And I'd sooner make tracks than try to spell things out." He got up, brushed off the dust. "You're a weird sort, you know. And you're welcome."

Softness, its traces, left. Her blood boiled. Ears tingled with blood pressure rising.

Bundling the mud-coated rope, he gave her one last head-to-toe look. "At least you're in one piece. Quite a sight to behold. I'll miss seeing you." He shook his head and turned to leave.

Maybe she'd misread him. No, she knew she'd misread him. No one did this to her. No one turned and left once she was ready to maybe give them another chance and maybe even fight for something that just might be worth fighting for. This did not happen to Professor Eve Sanchez.

Shit!

He was twenty or thirty steps off before Eve spoke up. "I'm sorry. Thank you. Maybe you're not the man I thought," she said with a bite. She wanted her words to dig in and make him flinch. She was angry and he could either take it or not.

He didn't turn around, the last of him vanishing amid scrub oak, majestic cottonwoods, and turquoise skies.

CHAPTER 14

Graciéla gently opened her eyes. It was as though she emerged from profound meditation. Memories of the yoga practice room of the bookstore lingered. Her life, now past, flickered like specters in the night.

The realm of her awakening sheltered her under a sky-blue atmosphere. What appeared to be a midmorning sun streamed but did not burn. She observed, waiting for her senses to acclimate, seeing as through white cotton sheers.

Slowly, her senses awoke. Sharp and clear, iridescent waves and particles of white, red, yellow, and blue light rolled across her field of vision. They danced playfully, streams of energy, pure and positive.

Eve's face flickered within her mind. Graciéla was quickened to things close at hand and far off, in this realm and in the world from which she had departed. Eve knew better than to trust a conniving man. She should not give him another chance, lessons from the past invaluable, hazardous to dismiss. Love was artistry. What appeared to be so often was not. Love might not be love. In the end, Eve must decide.

Votive candles sat atop a low-lying, ages-old piñon slab fixed on two large sandstone rocks. A cluster of granite stones from the Sandia Mountains formed a circle in front of a primal altar.

It was a place of conjuring, natural magic, nurturing the confluence of forces of earth, air, fire, water, and ether. It was what she had known on earth but lighter, somehow denser and purer.

Death had taken her by surprise. An old medicine woman from Aztlan del Norte, Francesca, had instructed a young Graciéla. *"It takes energy to be well just as it does to be ill. Do not deplete vital resources lest things take a turn."*

Graciéla saw the treachery that plotted Eve's demise. Behind everyday twists and turns was the force of a seasoned practitioner in the evil arts. The sacred space darkened. Gray clouds clustered overhead. A nefarious spirit watched and directed foul energy at an unsuspecting soul. It was aimed at Eve.

Graciéla straightened her spine. She remained a yogic adept. Feminine power coursed through her as an unobstructed electromagnetic force. She focused on Eve. *Harness your inner resources lest things take a turn.* Her mystic third eye burned and glowed white-hot. A formidable wielder of evil feminine magic was targeting Eve, and Eve was vulnerable.

Sweet Mary retreated to her bedroom, away from gawking eyes of neighbors shamed by her nudity. Nearly half an hour on her front porch in the fresh air, sheltered under an awning, had passed. It was more than enough time to plot the day's intrigues.

Each day brought its surprises. Today dripped with delicious cunning. Sam's antics made the scheming easy.

She sat on her bed to read the morning newspaper. Images of Sam intruded on her mind as she flipped from page to page. It was annoying to be consumed by this man. Never had any male so demanded her attention. Waking thoughts and dreams were of him. She preferred her mind clear, able to strategize delightful misdeeds.

Sweet Mary intuited what Sam did. She sensed his whereabouts and doings as electricity before a storm. Against her will, he'd gone to the bosque. Sweet Mary's intuition picked up on the misdeed. Immediately, she superimposed on his mind the image of taunting and teasing the challenger bitch.

Pulling the bitch out of the quicksand with the rope was Sweet Mary's idea. Sam had seen Sweet Mary's reflection in the surface of the quicksand. Anything could morph into a looking glass when a black-magic witch willed it.

Sam saw Sweet Mary and heard the instruction. He was to inch out of the mud the contender for Sam, the Sweet Mary Made Man. Then, seconds before delivering her to safety, he'd toss her headfirst back into the bowels of the gurgling wet earth.

Sam resisted Sweet Mary, refused his psychic mother. He did what he'd never done before. He'd defied her wishes. Sweet Mary didn't tolerate defiance. She dealt severely with bald-faced defiers. Blood pressure rising, her ears tingled with red-hot hate.

She left her bed and went to her huge, mirror-lined bathroom. Mirrors transfixed her. They were portals to hidden dimensions. People didn't consider what happened when they looked into mirrors, what and whom they might see if they really believed in magic.

Steam covered the walls as the double-headed shower ran full blast with hot water. It was her custom to leave the water blasting hot as the worst day in hell for a full ten minutes. Then she'd step into the bathroom, into the realm of seeing. Steam fully coated the mirrors.

The hot water tank continually replenished its store, energy and matter manipulated with a flick of a pissed-off witch's will. Staring into the misted looking glass allowed her to see into the soul of her kept one. She saw Sam in the bosque. Private detectives had tipped him off about the female contender's whereabouts. She'd gone to the forest to think things through, and that's when Sweet Mary decided to trip into the paranormal scene and inflict unexpected wizardry. The *bosque* was also Sam's place to visit, where he went to be alone, away from Sweet Mary's influence—so he thought.

Sweet Mary in the steamed glass had been refused. Sweet Mary had been betrayed. *De la muerte y de la suerte nadie se escape.* She muttered, "Death and destiny, no one can avoid." Laughter escaped from her mouth like denizens of crazed mothers whose sons had violated their oath to the woman who had given them everything. Craning her head back, she howled with outrage.

Seconds, hours, or eons passed. Time did not matter in the world of witches and sordid magic. Sweet Mary continued to gaze into the bathroom mirror, its surface dripping with humidity. She pondered and plotted, scene after terrible scene supernaturally forming across the hazy glass.

At her making, Sam had become a veritable male deity.

What he would lose for his wanton ways would take him by gruesome surprise. His own tormented childhood had left him a decayed semblance of a man, weak and ill-tempered. Moody men were souls lost to a mother's needs and demands. They never were what mothers needed them to be. Moreover, primal needs had never been met.

Sam was ripe for the witchy picking. He was caught in the listless ways of addiction and despair. Suicide would have been his end. But Sweet Mary, Michté, Queen of Mictlan, Goddess of the Aztlan underworld and afterlife, discovered her Mictécli. The old god of ancient lore, Mictécli (dba Sam Shear) would stand guard over Michté and her business and legal concerns.

Sweet Mary saw potential in his bloodshot eyes, miserable and jaded with flickers of rage that hadn't died out. Mr. World-Weary and Gutter-Worn Sam Shear was down and out but could be shaped. He was destined to rule by the side of Sweet Mary, queen of underworld perversions and loveless lives.

The day before discovering Sam, Sweet Mary had been released from the Aztlan del Sur County Psychiatric Hospital. Antipsychotic drugs lingered in her system after forced injections during her month-long stay. Her mind was cloudy but malicious, nonetheless.

Sweet Mary had the wherewithal to will Sam Shear to life.

Sweet Mary had her own terrorizing history with the law. She'd been hospitalized by court order due to the legal wheeling and dealing of a sleazy but rich businessman whom Sweet Mary had threatened. He'd refused her thousand-dollar hourly fee. He scoffed and before closing her bedroom door, spit on the carpet. She curled a pointed index finger and intoned a witch's curse as her blue eyes shifted to black.

"Bagabi laca lama sabathani! *Bagabi laca lama sabathani!* *Bagabi laca lama sabathani!"* Sweet Mary had screamed the curse.

Wild-eyed, the slimy patron fled, called in political favors, and had Sweet Mary hospitalized. Before her release, scumbag businessman was dead, having succumbed to lethal carbon dioxide fumes. Tipped-off newsmen discovered him naked by his mistress's side in the penthouse of downtown's most luxurious hotel. Sweet Mary's curses flew and took.

In the shadowy alleyway twelve years ago, Sweet Mary had whispered in Sam's ear. She'd offered, "Come to me. Be mine. And you will be as a god." Passed his mouthful of drool and vomit, he muttered something Sweet Mary took as an assent.

Twelve years to the day, the slumping pathetic figure of days past did the unthinkable. He forgot the vow to Sweet Mother Mary. Vows to Sweet Mary were not forgotten. A thrill lit up her spine and to the center of her forehead. She relished retribution.

Sam would pay.

CHAPTER 15

T hey drove up the paved road to Sam's high-desert hacienda at the base of the Sandia Mountain foothills. He'd come back into the forest for Eve with a blanket in hand. "Staying in wet and grimy clothes is no good," he'd said. She'd taken his advice and gone behind the scrub oak and a stand of trees to change.

They approached the entrance of his home. Eve was struck by the surreal appearance of the place. It appeared to grow out of desert sand and granite, outsized as the man himself. A massive brown expanse, it hugged the earth as an adobe fortress, obtruding against a cloudless turquoise- blue sky and ancient boulder-strewn eastern foothills.

Three stories of sunbaked, brown mud and straw plastered with exquisite earth tones exuded an arrogant presence. Driving along a carefully grated packed-earth road, Eve's skin crawled. The region felt unhallowed. Her fingernails dug into the thickly padded, leather seat of the plush BMW.

Sam shot her a sideways glance and chuckled. He'd

explained the quality and cost of the automobile the second Eve stepped in and gasped. The same braggadocio spirit curled out of his mouth as they approached the monstrous desert abode. "Don't worry, it's bigger than it looks. Last time, you were here at night. Noonday sun and it grows." He flushed and laughed softly.

Eve was conflicted. His switch between arrogance and sincerity were tantalizing. She never knew what to expect. The prospect of trouble loomed, and it didn't bother her. She rubbed the tips of her fingers across her forehead and tried to clear her mind.

They approached the end of the driveway at the front of the home. Window sashes and wood trim painted turquoise ran the circumference of the hacienda. It was surprising since Native lore held that turquoise warded off evil spirits. Sam was arrogant, and arrogance was a wicked thing taught the Native peoples of Aztlan. Turquoise as warding, turquoise as hope.

Parking the spotless car between a thirty-foot spread of sandstone pillars, Sam turned to her. "I hope you approve." He didn't wait for an answer before getting out to open her door.

Anxiously, Eve stepped out.

The splendor of granite mountains bordering the historic Turquoise Trail between Aztlan del Sur and Aztlan del Norte, a windless atmosphere, and total silence felt strange, eerie.

At a mile and a half high, the view was breathtaking as the eye drifted to the west for over one hundred miles to an ancient volcano deemed sacred by local Pueblos. To the north, reigned the Sangre de Cristo Mountain Range of Aztlan del Norte. The sky burned the purest of blues. Without sunglasses, Eve needed to shield her eyes.

Sam came up from behind and placed a hand on her shoulder, his touch sure and oddly comforting. Yet, Eve stiffened.

"Reserved. I get it. Things take time." He stepped back, gentlemanly. "Let's go inside, and you can take off that blanket and get into comfortable clothes."

They walked toward the twelve-foot-tall carved oak front doors. Quetzalcoatl, feathered serpent god of Aztlan, wings spread triumphantly, and the Mayan sun god were carved into waxed wood. She stopped and grazed her fingertips over the relief carving. In an instant, the feathers of the deity appeared to flutter and the rays of the sun god stretch outward. She gasped and drew back. Sam gently touched the small of her back. He smiled and nodded at the carvings.

She looked and the door of the feathered serpent had become the image of the sun god and the other door the god-ruler of Aztlan, Quetzalcoatl.

She felt disoriented, her knees buckling slightly. He placed the palm of his hand now firmly against her back. "You'll be all right. Let's get you changed and comfortable."

At the river, she'd taken off her muddy clothes and wrapped herself in the blanket. Eve told him where she lived, and Sam said they were closer to his house by freeway time. She protested as Sam opened the passenger door of his car and she slid in. Sam drove toward the freeway, said a favor for a favor. He'd saved her life. Time in return wasn't too much to ask, long or short, up to her. He shot onto the entrance ramp, not waiting for a reply.

He opened the double doors, bowed, and swept his right arm and hand gallantly for Eve to enter. She walked forward and gasped as she entered the vaulted entryway. Soaring clearstory walls jutted up to twenty-foot ceilings that framed the Sandia Mountains. Gazing upward, Eve found purchase with the bannister of the spiraling oaken stairway.

Sam had disappeared. Eve looked around. His abode teemed with energy, vital and expansive.

There was a spiritual cast along the white interior adobe walls, a light shimmer from sun and bees-waxed plaster. It felt similar to the numinous vortices of the Four Corners area of Aztlan, the quadripoint of psychic energies for the mestizos of the southwestern United States.

From her studies, she knew psychic energy could be used for good or bad. Practitioners of the left-hand path of magic exploited it for gain. They confiscated the energy of others for sustenance and to perform unconscionable deeds. Eve had memorized lines from one of the major teachers of black magic. She had recited the text to her university class.

Always remember, wherever you are, whether near or far, you had a mother who really, really loved you. The original mother. She is the one who nurtures you and corrects you if you are misguided.

Trouble was, Eve informed her students, mothers could be good or bad. Symbols revealed a two-sided issue when it came to mothers. They could be nurturing or devouring. They helped or they hurt. When they hurt, they could commit atrocities. The mother of the left-hand path was a malignant spirit written about in both ancient Eastern and Western mystical texts.

Myths of the crazed mother abounded in Aztlan. *La Dolores* morphed into a frightful owl, terrorizing men indebted to her until one of those men took out his rifle and killed the owl with a shot through the eye. The dead bird was found with the right eye blown out, left wing extended and nearly ripped off, and the left foot doubled up under the little corpse. Later that day, La Dolores was discovered lying on the floor of her home with a bullet through her right eye, left arm raised and almost torn off, and her foot twisted hideously against her chest.

Sam reappeared from around a six-foot-tall granite fireplace at the far end of the entryway and great room. Behind it, lay a gleaming hallway of highly polished gray granite.

"Sorry, I needed to tend to something. Hope you weren't lonely." Sincerity couldn't be doubted, smooth as spider silk. "Please, follow me, and I'll show you to where you can shower and change into dry clothes. Then, I'll fix us lunch."

Impressive. Fixes lunch to boot. She walked across the elegantly furnished great room, fine beige leathers and expensive Navajo carpets softening the hard-edged granite fireplace and sandstone floors. Turning down a long and windowless hallway, Eve noticed shadows wavering then disappearing. Antique bronze wall sconces provided subdued lighting. Interspersed were red votive candles set in adobe *nichos*, recesses carved into the wall. Flickers from passing shadows felt like more than plays of light and dark. A chill went up her spine.

Frosted glass double doors stood at the end of the forty-foot-long hallway. Sam opened the door, held it for Eve. Humidity filled the air. She crossed the threshold, skin tingling, breathing easier even as her mind lingered on the hallway shadows.

Sam apparently noticed her beginning to relax. "I thought spending some time in here would help." He pointed to the oversized jacuzzi, bubblers set. Fragrances of aloe and lavender wafted through her lungs. "The dry sauna is over here." They walked about to a cedar door behind which was a sauna. "I'll give you your privacy. Take your time. I'll be outside doing laps in the swimming pool." He motioned to a clear glass door. A sandstone-paved walkway led to a black lap pool. It shimmered like obsidian under the high-noon sun.

"Black pool?"

"Special paint called Southwest obsidian black. It's wonderful at night under cloudless skies, and stars spread out like a blanket. It's strangely pacifying."

He opened the sliding door to the pool. They walked to the iridescent water. She stood at the edge of the pool. It appeared depthless—unsettling.

An urge to shed the light blanket and dive into the black pool tugged. It was an odd compulsion. She recalled standing at the edge of the Grand Canyon and wanting to step off. The words of T.S. Eliot, quoted to students, came to mind,

O, dark dark dark. They all go into the dark, the vacant interstellar spaces, the vacant into the vacant... I said to my soul, be still.

She stepped back.

Sam reached to the side and gently touched her shoulder. "You all right?"

"I think I'll go back inside." She turned and walked away. Memories of a little girl stirred. She was abandoned by her father and neglected by a desperate mother. She was lost in a dark forest. She was running along the banks of the Rio Grande, trying to find her way back home.

By nightfall, tension had dissipated. Hours had whisked by at the hacienda of Sam Shear, conversation smooth as two roadrunners along a high-desert plateau. Subjects switched between politics and culture, neither hesitating in their strong opinions. Sam wasn't as smooth as he appeared. He had rough spots, more unrefined than met the casual eye. His arguments blistered with generalities. He'd become flustered with Eve's precision of thought, and then back off, knowing a silver-tongued barrister had been bested.

He prepared a dinner of grilled, wild-caught Alaskan salmon and tossed an arugula salad with olive oil, lemon, and Parmesan cheese with other assorted mixed greens from his garden. On Saturdays, he tended his raised beds of arugula, lettuce, carrots, tomatoes, and a variety of chiles. The man had intriguing talents. Eve watched contentedly as she sipped a glass of pinot grigio.

Nearing nine p.m., dinner finished and dishes washed, they sat comfortably in front of the poolside. Piñon and cedar logs blazed and crackled in the outdoor fireplace. The air breathed a mile-and-a-half high clean and crisp.

Earlier in the afternoon, Sam had dismissed the household staff so he and Eve could spend time alone. Crossed-legged, yoga style on billowy beige oversized canvas pillows, they enjoyed an after-dinner glass of summer peach wine from Aztlan del Sur's St. Clair Winery. Eve wore a pair of Sam's loose, white linen yoga pants, rolled up and cinched at the waist with a warm cotton shirt of well-worn softness.

The man was a conundrum, a confusing mess beneath a polished exterior. Her appraisal of the downtown lawyer had been tempered. Relaxing talk, a fine meal, and fine libations paved the way for character, charm, and concern. She'd been drawn into the spell of a mixed-bag man.

Sam reached for her hand, electricity pulsing through Eve's core. Heat built and throbbed. Feelings grew intense as fireplace flames licked upward. Images of drawing close, into Sam's embrace, swirled through her mind.

She felt drunk and hoped it didn't show. She was man-drunk, and man-drunk always turned into a wild ride. Goddess beckoned. Memories of other men flashed to consciousness. Eve didn't want a repeat.

She tightened up. Sam felt it. He turned from his lounging position and looked at her, didn't say anything, simply watched. She took a deep breath. The outside air drew dry and pure. She let go of Sam's hand and stretched back on the body-sized canvas pillow, black sky arching overhead like an indomitable yet benevolent god.

Eve heard the chanting of her people. Pueblo Natives danced under full-moon radiance and intoned songs to earth, air, fire, and water. Eve closed her eyes, drifted into a dreamlike realm.

She stood, shed her clothes, and slipped into the black shimmering water. Warmth caressed her body. She swam, and as she reached the end of the pool, she turned and looked back at Sam who lay at the far side, transfixed.

"Are you happy?" His voice was forty feet away but sounded as if he had whispered in her ear.

"I am happy." A falling star streaked across the overhead sky, disappearing into the distance.

CHAPTER 16

Next morning, university life jolted Eve into everyday academic realities. Her nerves were set on edge the second she'd stepped out of her car and onto campus. The angst of university life couldn't be bypassed in spite of last night's pleasures.

Bickering, strategizing, backstabbing, and subtle undermining peppered the halls of the University of Aztlan. She despised pretentious academics and the toxic subterfuge of the academy. She'd have left, found a different scholarly gig, were it not for the love of teaching. Devotion to her students kept her in her challenging job.

She looked out at the empty lecture auditorium. The fifty-minute class had ended with a discussion of the final rites of shamanic burial rituals. No longer than forty hours after the final breath, the luminous body was released, negative energies dispelled via magical visualizations.

Students sat mesmerized by Eve's vast knowledge and passion for her research. Burial rituals made for alluring academic lectures since they entered into ancient mysteries fortified by Eve's personal experiences with shamanism in Aztlan. Scholarly residencies honed her knowledge.

She had lived and studied with female shamans in Aztlan del Norte and Aztlan del Sur. They were aged curanderas specializing in rituals for healing and death. Out of her studies and experience, she'd written an academically acclaimed book titled *Aztlan Shamanism: Portal to Unseen Worlds*.

Packed classes of one hundred or more were typical for Eve's lectures. The year before last, she'd been voted most popular professor on campus. Students flocked semester after semester to erudite teachings about myth, mystery, and the occult.

Eve missed Sam. Memories of the sun's arch over the tip of the Sandia Mountains streaming through the clearstory of Sam's guest bedroom brought a smile. She'd spent the night in the arms of the most intriguing and frightening of men. He was enticing, the attraction and sense of danger irresistible.

Sam had transformed from brash and harsh downtown lawyer at a seedy bar to a refined gentleman. Sincerity and warmth were lavished as smoothly as exotic oils on weather-beaten skin. After the night's swim, they had made their way toward the intimacy of the master suite, high-desert stars twinkling magnificently through spotless windows.

Dreams flickered through the night—erotic images of sensitively rendered passion. However, even within the dream world, Eve's lucid mind awoke. She wondered, doubted. No man with such a vicious underside could be so loving.

Perhaps she had projected onto Sam what she wanted and needed. Perhaps love would fade. Perhaps she'd settle for what she could get. *"Bad love is better than no love."* Shirley's words made her flinch, a pit in her stomach yawning.

Eve finished packing her notes into her scarred, brown leather satchel. She fantasized of Sam's well-defined body, contour and muscles distinct as a Michelangelo sculpture. Warmth flushed through her body. An electrical current streamed to her center and made a descent. She shuddered.

A scream from the back of the lecture hall shocked her out of the fantasy. Her head jerking upward, she saw a woman. At the back door, an assailant, a male, threw the student to the ground.

Eve ran up the steps and toward the girl. She appeared unconscious. The attacker was gone as was the girl's purse. Students from the hallways entered the auditorium and gathered. They nodded and snickered, pointed to the girl's limp body. Eve didn't understand their cruelty.

"Call security... and 911. Let's get some help here." At first, no one responded then a few of the students pulled out their cell phones, a couple of others dashing off for security. Eve brushed the girl's hair away from her neck and face, felt a pulse at her carotid. She knew better than to try to turn her on her back. She didn't know how badly she'd been hurt.

Her breath was rank, startling Eve. She drew back. In Aztlan culture, breath betrayed the spirit, illness and wickedness associated with foul odor. Aztlan natives believed Ehacatl-Quetzalcoatl emanated from the breath of the god, Tonacatecuhtli. Breath spirit signaled the nature of the spirit.

Eve's heart rate picked up, and her mouth became dry. Things weren't as they appeared. She wondered about the real story here, perhaps something students knew about. Suddenly, the girl flew up to a sitting position, eyes wide and bright. Eve drew back. Each of the twenty-five or thirty people in the semicircle pulled away. Silence, electric and raw, pierced the atmosphere.

The girl, like an automaton, gazed at each person then screamed viciously. Guttural sounds, grating and mean, emanated from the petite and wan student. Multiple terrorizing voices, legions of demoniacs, cursed from within her. They screamed in unintelligible dialects.

Then, pointing a sharp, black index fingernail at Eve, she shrieked, "From the four winds of the dark abyss, I curse you! *Bagabi laca lama sabathani. Bagabi laca lama sabathani. Bagabi laca lama sabathani.*" She finished, eyes rolling to the back of her head, and fainted once again. Eve reached out and cradled her head with her hand before it hit the cement floor.

Students, ears cupped against the shrill sound, stepped back, dumbfounded. They caught each other's eyes and shook their heads in disbelief. Half of those gathered, ran off, peering back before exiting the auditorium for a last look at the hideous student turned tormented creature. The others stood paralyzed.

Eve couldn't move. The words—*Bagabi laca lama sabathani*—echoed through her mind. From research, she knew the terrible intent of the words. She'd been cursed.

A few seconds later, she was alone. Everyone had either drifted out or scattered.

Witches of Aztlan used the incantation to conjure mischief and evil. They could do it from a distance, take possession of an already crazed mind. Words would fly out of the mouth of the victim's soul. The curse would be laid and set without the presence of the witch.

Eve had studied the history of Aztlan incantations. They conjured up foul energy that hurt people. Few saw the malicious force coming. There was no way to prepare or prevent it. Good luck turned bad. People fell ill. Love ended before it took root. In all manner of things, good was stopped and bad set loose.

The meaning of the words was unknown save to that one infamous witch of Aztlan, Michté, who spewed them. They issued from her wicked spirit. The curse, when it stuck, stuck, and there was no escape. It bore down and into the soul, viciously and deep. Men and women never recovered. Many went insane, loss of love and hope forever relegating the mind to lunacy.

Eve knew words carried power. They accessed dark spiritual powers. And it was the intent behind the utterances that inflicted damage. Malicious intent mixed with strong emotion conjured foul deeds and life-threatening afflictions.

The girl's emotion had run white hot. She had a bad spirit that directed hatred at Eve. Eve felt disoriented, tingling moving through arms and legs. Her stomach was queasy, and the room faded in and out. Nausea made its way from stomach to throat, a metallic taste washing through her mouth. She shook her head.

Graciéla came. Her imaged flickered beside Eve. *The incantation has no power unless the soul is vulnerable.* Eve knew vulnerability came from excessive tiredness, stress, and yielding to despair. She sat on the cold, gray concrete floor and pulled her knees tight against her stomach, her back against the wall.

The world faded. Eve closed her eyes, and the drums of the Pueblo medicine people began beating. She swayed, a spirit in the desert with her mother's medicine people dancing, chanting, and smudging her with the smoke of dried sage, an antidote to dispel evil.

Sam had returned to his hacienda after taking Eve home. There was a lightness to his step that hadn't been there in years. Victories in the court were no match for this kind of feeling.

He retreated to his study, stretched out on the reclining, blue leather swivel chair behind his expansive cherry wood desk. His eyes roamed over the scores of bells, shells, and macaw feathers collected from various trips to the Mesoamerican motherland. The realm spoke to him of soulful things and mystic ponderings of mind.

He had told no one of this sensitivity. But he felt that the time of such guardedness might be coming to an end. A solitary and fractious heart sensed life in the balance.

Under glass, he stored two eggs at the perfect temperature. The blue egg, at the northern corner of the large library, sat positioned atop a white four-foot limestone pedestal. A brown egg also enclosed in shatterproof glass was situated on a similar limestone block in front of the westernmost sandstone window ledge.

Acoma tales state that men must choose between two paths in life, one the way of the macaw, the other that of the crow. The macaw symbolized the ability to listen to one's inner voice and evolve. The crow's representation was that of a guilt-free predator. No one knew which way he or she would choose. Events played out. Each person chose his or her path, that of the lustrous blue egg or mottled brown egg.

He thought about Eve. She was a woman of intelligence, sensitivity, and beauty. His home had impressed her. He hoped *he* had. It wasn't clear since she could prove difficult to read, her ways often enigmatic. It wasn't her admiration he cared about. The need to impress had vanished once they'd sat cozily on overstuffed pillows in front of the fire. What he desired was true affection. He hoped for this, and such hope was new for one not prone to tender considerations.

Moonglow on a cloudless night, he thought of her without clothes beside the pool. She and the night were one. Darkness wrapped itself around her form, and Sam was both soothed and aroused. Thoughts of Eve were nearly as delicious as the woman herself.

Last night, hours had passed like a few minutes. Conversation flowed, relaxation and attraction grew steadily as mountain streams gaining force from a spring thaw. Sam wanted to be with her.

He remembered how she casually touched his hand after he'd told a particularly funny joke or related how he'd been able to offer legal assistance gratis. Even men considered a bane had their light side. The trouble was, Sam wasn't sure about his light side, whether it was real or not, whether it could be trusted.

She challenged him and said his pro bono work seemed ego driven, a man desperate for public approval making efforts to be liked. Sam recalled squinting and flinching at her remark. It caused him to ponder. He raised one eyebrow then the other. Then he didn't answer, didn't need to, simply smiled.

She gave a quick flip of her long, auburn hair and moved past his silence, changed the subject to the outdoors, hiking, snowshoeing, rafting. They spoke of the places they'd visited in Aztlan, the highest peaks climbed, the trails snow shoed, the dreams they'd had while camping under the stars in the mountains of northern Aztlan. She'd been surprised at their love for nature and need for time alone. Sam enjoyed talking of their similarities, chemistry intensifying as they spoke.

Talk led to touch and soon there were no more words. They spent the night together. He relished memories of her body, the curves, folds, and taste. Eve was an intoxicating woman.

The room spun pleasantly.

A hand grabbed the back of Sam's chair, nearly toppled him to the floor. A spasm shot through to his lower back. "What the hell!" He forced away the pain and shot up to his feet. Chair springs bent and cried out under the strain.

A woman cackled. Her voice was unmistakable as nails down a chalkboard. Stealthily, she'd come up from behind, through the secret outside passage that Sam had installed when he built the home three years ago. Sweet Mary was the only one who knew about it and used it. She refused to be encumbered by staff answering the front door, and then having to walk the long hallway to Sam's lair. She'd told him to construct a secret entrance.

"Sammy Boy!" Sweet Mary, with her perfectly coiffed platinum-blonde hair, stood over him. Her arms were cocked to the side. She acted as if she owned the place. It infuriated him. A flare of temper was masked. He gagged it with a quick grit of the teeth.

Floor-to-ceiling expensive leather-bound volumes of classic literature appeared as mere wallpaper against Sweet Mary's formidable presence. She smacked her Chiclets the way a renegade militia fires Uzi submachine guns into a crowd. The annoyance of it was a malodorous scent, brief and passing. He dared not betray his repulsion lest he offend one he could not afford to live without.

Sweet Mary had her own key to Sam's place, but it didn't

matter since he rarely locked the doors. He was on his own acreage with an electronically controlled wrought-iron gate fronting the property. She knew the code and just about everything else about Sam, including the private passage and private goings-on that never escaped her hypervigilant eye.

She swiped the tip of one long finger along the edges of the cherry wood bookcase that ran alongside his desk. She moved to the front of the expansive piece of imported furniture, gaze cold and piercing. Her way was sly and silky, not to be trifled with lest a man be undone quicker than an Aztlan mud puddle dries up under the high-noon sun.

Everywhere she went, men turned her way, nearly fell off their barstools, or stumbled on the sidewalk. When she entered the room or passed by, they knew that they had visually encountered the most vicious of feline creatures.

She had smoldering, lusty good looks that betrayed a woman skilled in her craft and knowledgeable in things that the common female never hazarded to guess. Her reputation in Aztlan superseded the nastiest of Wild West barflies. Nice rack, firm ass, and round in all the right places, Sam's notorious acquaintances jested when caught in a liquor-induced haze and mind fog that obscured the danger of speaking without respect about a vengeful woman.

A lump formed in Sam's throat at Sweet Mary's presence and harsh bravado. He hated feeling squeamish. She picked up on things, had the sensitivity of the most infamous of West Mesa serial killers, who did their deeds and buried the remains inconspicuously along abandoned desert arroyos. Any trace of self-doubt weakened Sam's standing with her. He knew she held the cards and knew how to deal them.

Sweet Mary's devilish power oozed from a finely sharpened mind and was never to be minimized or dismissed.

The lump in his throat always came when Sweet Mary was up to something surprising and unsettling. And she was always up to something surprising and unsettling. She came to his home when she needed Sam's expertise, appropriate legal maneuvering. Sam had never let her down, never would, because Sweet Mary made him what he was. Without her, it would be back to not winning a single legal case no matter how trivial and simple. Littered downtown alleyways would once again become Sam's home stinking home.

"Sammy? You feeling better?" She smiled with her knowing smile. She'd dipped into his secrets. How she knew, what she knew, was nothing he could guess. He grew weak-kneed and hoped it didn't show. She'd bring him to his knees and keep him there. She hated weakness. She taught him to be fierce, demanded that he stay that way.

Sweet Mary's voice was laced with threat. It was violating. Everything about her violated him. It was a wonder there was anything left of him, a self—a soul. He stayed quiet. Silence was best when he'd been caught off guard. Explanations were senseless against she who knew all.

She saw right through him. There was no escape. But he didn't have to say so. He kept his own mind.

A sick feeling twisted like gut rot churning down and around into an empty stomach. There was no retreat. A ruthless lawyer needed to save his own ass. This was a definite untoward predicament.

"What's her name?" Red lipstick adorned her porcelain skin. Sweet Mary walked around the desk, back toward Sam. She knew Eve's name just as she knew everything, but she wanted to force words out of Sam. Humbling a man was Sweet Mary's delight.

His left eye twitched. He placed a hand on the edge of his

desk. She spotted it, the twitch.

She was a rabid forest feline targeting wounded prey. She moved forward. She smiled. She was silent.

Trickles of sweat ran down Sam's temples. Blue eyes bore artic cold into Sam's mind. Sweat curled onto lips. Sweet Mary stroked her right index finger across Sam's right cheek, past beads of sweat then went down the front of his open-shirted chest. She dug in, twisted chest hairs, penetrated skin. He bled.

Anguish made things pass slowly. Pain crept like trains of desert turtles winding through rocky arroyos. A tortured mind was a wearisome suffering. Sweet Mary's twirling metal-cold index finger rent its way farther into chest hair and flesh. She tugged the graying hairs. Her eyes were riveted on Sam as she ripped patches of hair out of chest. Searing pain.

He didn't wince. He dragged it inside. He snuffed it out. It died quickly.

"Asked a question, Sam. Answer. Goddammit." Snarls jettisoned out of a madwoman's throat. Dungeons of specters intoned their way out of the downtown witch's voice box.

Words were trapped in Sam's mouth. He'd locked them up and didn't want them leaking out. He feared what he'd say if he let loose. There'd be no taking anything back because you can't pull back what's meant to hit and wreck. He wanted to undo and ruin Sweet Mary. He'd always wanted to.

No one had ever gotten to Sweet Mary. If they tried, she made them pay. It was always bloody bad. They wished they never set eyes on Aztlan's downtown bitch *bruja*. They cried out for death. She was a fearsome thing.

They never saw it coming. It undid them. Manhood was stripped and filleted. She started with the mind, and they'd scream because of the voices in their head that drowned out everything pleasing and good, leaving them raw and tortured. Nothing happened on the outside since this was an inside-the-mind game that ate away at stability and sanity sure as termites on river wood. She worked inside out, tailings toxic. A dead and bloodied body was the cherry on top of this bruja's violence festival party cake.

She intuited Sam's intent. Her blue eyes glistened. A smile, the slightly turned-up corners of her mouth. The red witch tongue moistened barely parted lips.

He pulled back his malice. He knew he could call it up again when things were safer. He had no intention of becoming a wasteland corpse.

"You know, Sammy..."

He hated *Sammy*. His mother called him Sammy. She knew it and did it with a look that made him shrivel.

He'd hated his mother. He hated Sweet Mary, she who scooped him up when he'd been a gutter rat goner. Mother emptied him, by her needs and demands. She was a woman who took and never stopped the taking. Sweet Mary was a woman who gave and never stopped demanding back.

Sam never spoke about his mother, never spoke about childhood, no need. It was locked tight. Best to leave it bundled and gagged.

Sweet Mary heard the tossing and rumbling of the bundle. Her eyes glinted. Her smile widened. She was mother love gone bad. He needed to keep his mouth shut. He needed to keep his mind shut. He needed to blank out and go away.

Sam smiled.

Sweet Mary squeezed his shoulder muscle with an iron-like left hand. "Through the years, none of those women troubled me," she asserted with a wink and a nod. She snapped her gum, sounded like a wild cat smacking meat.

"This one's different. So Sammy, careful—'cuz you know who you belong to. Don't forget."

Sweet Mary leaned forward and kissed him with parted lips.

CHAPTER 17

Back home, Eve dressed for an evening out. Early afternoon, Sam called and said he couldn't stand to be away from her. He asked her out, and without pause, she accepted. She hadn't been with a man for six months. Another date with Sam Shear was thrill enough to make up for too many lonely months. *Too much aloneness makes for its own kind of crazy.* She was done trying to dodge the inevitable.

She and Sam had a chance. She could feel it, and she'd go with it. She wanted to ride it through.

Trust was a big thing. Damaged in childhood and trying to grow trust back was like trying to water the desert with a garden hose. Warmth flushed head to toe. She knew she was falling in love. Maybe it was too quick. But when the land was parched…

Intuitive warnings kept flickering in the background. She'd keep them in mind. Things needed to be given a chance. She was excited.

Afternoon air had turned a harsh autumn cold. Outside

her bedroom window, winds whipped through the street and blew tumbleweeds in zigzagging patterns like crazed devils on the loose. Strewn debris littered her desert-landscaped front yard. Branches of the forty-year-old elm tree in the center of the yard bent under the pressure of fierce, early evening winds.

The day had passed quickly, chock-full of surprises. The crazed student had been rushed to the Behavioral Health Care Unit of Downtown Aztlan Hospital. She suffered from a history of mental instability, chronic paranoid schizophrenia, and heard malicious voices. Nevertheless, spouting out the exact words of the witch's ages-old curse was nothing short of remarkable and worrisome.

Levied at Eve, the curse hit like a jolt of electricity from fingertips to heart. Molten lava raged downward and into her core. She had given no sign of consternation. She remembered Graciéla's teaching about curses only taking effect if the soul was vulnerable. She'd closed off her mind and heart. She was good at closing off.

She knew who was behind the curse. This was a first. Up till now, there'd been only normal foes, envious colleagues, and old flames of past lovers. None had ever packed this kind of psychic punch.

The afternoon had gone by, university business tended to, late afternoon yoga fitted in. But nothing proved as mind and body relieving and restoring as the thought of a fine man with the right woman on his mind.

Sam said he'd pick her up at seven thirty. That gave her time to get home from a hard-pressed day, shower, and dress for dinner. They had reservations at Aztlan's reigning upscale restaurant, the Artichoke Cafe. It was a see-and-be-seen place with an exquisite reputation for culinary mastery.

Sam had dropped her off at home that morning, said he could hardly wait to be with her again. He was warm and sincere. It made Eve's heart melt. She teared and quickly wiped it away and hoped he hadn't noticed.

From a cedar-lined closet, she took out a black silk evening dress, its smoothness cool to the touch. Friends said expensive fabric and curve-hugging design accentuated a luxurious feline's grace and charms, and no man ever failed to steal a glance or two or three.

It was ten past seven. Dress slipped on. It draped down—sumptuous, touchable, and fine.

There was a secret beneath the man. It spoke to a story few knew or guessed. She sensed she was gaining entrance and that the going was not assured. He was a strong man keen on hiding even traces of emotion and openness. Yet, he'd been tender, and she sensed there was room for more.

Eve opened then closed her hose drawer. They weren't necessary, legs a natural bronze. Zipping up the back of the dress, she relished thoughts of what the evening might hold in store. Images of Sam stirred her senses, kindled vivid memories and fantasies. She sat on the edge of the bed, caught her breath, and tried to focus. She needed to finish dressing. She wanted to be in one piece and present as a put-together woman.

Her knees refused to cease trembling. Leg muscles felt liquid, inner thighs twitching despite efforts to relax. Eve didn't get nerves on dates, but this was a date the way the Fourth of July in DC was a corner fireworks show.

The doorbell rang. Nerves jumped and sparked. The clock read seven thirty. Right on time.

Dizziness descended as she stood up. She got to the front door, didn't remember her steps to get there. She didn't want to turn the doorknob. There was a weird pull back. Her hand trembled.

He's just another guy like all the other guys. Bad boys never bring good. A seared conscience was a hard thing to curb.

Heartbeats pounded through her inner ear. Her hands were sweaty; her mouth turned sandstorm dry. Swallowing hard, she wanted to skip the date, open the door, and lie. She'd say she was sick. She *was* sick. Things never worked with men. Another bad time would kill her. She and men were a bad mix. Time to close it down.

Eve nearly flung the door open. Allure dripped, irresistible magnetism. Six-foot-two blue-eyed guys wrapped like this weren't an everyday occurrence. Her head spun, lightness trickled into mind and body. No words.

She flushed. Lights shot out from the periphery of her vision. Nausea curled then settled. She touched the doorframe, caught hold of herself, eyes closing then opening quickly.

Sam reached out and touched her shoulder. Immediately, it calmed her. He let out a large-hearted laugh. "Well, you all right?"

Eve gave a quick nod. There was nothing to say. Energy flowed quick and unobstructed.

Doubt skipped out, vanished.

"Well, you going to let me in or just stand there looking like a young girl on her first date?" The man looked delicious. Words sidled from gut to tongue. "Ah... ah... my gosh. Come in. I... I'm so sorry. It's just... you're devilishly handsome." The words spun out without censor.

Sam chuckled, stepped inside, and kissed her on the cheek. His eyes traveled up and down her silk-wrapped frame. "You look incredible."

A few seconds lapsed.

Sam shook his head, cleared his throat, and continued a soft gaze. He smelled fresh like autumn rain. Reaching into an elegantly tailored, blue-linen coat pocket, he presented a tiny gold box. It was wrapped with an ethereally thin, delicate blue ribbon. It glowed an unearthly hue of shimmering gray.

Eve was stunned. She reached out and took hold of the box. Running her fingers over it, she looked up at Sam. Strange currents, icy sharp, pulsated from the tiny container. "This didn't belong to Pandora, did it?" The tiny thing was bad.

Sam put his hand around her waist and pulled her close, lips almost touching. "If it did, I didn't know it." He tried to override her seriousness.

Coldness crept through Eve. Her right forearm throbbed. Frigid air chilled the living room. The thrill of seconds earlier died. She gave the box back to Sam.

Sam was surprised. He became mute, solemn, and remote. Features turned brittle. A terrible radiance emanated from the tiny container. Sam's countenance dulled to gray, downcast, and surly. Short-tempered meanness laced through harshly cut features, blues eyes stone hard, jaw muscles protruding, hands tensed into fists.

He shook his head sharply a couple of times. It wasn't clear to whom the anger was directed, toward Eve or an invisible other. Eye twitches thinly masked disgust and a seething violence.

He could erupt. Facial skin tightened to exert an awful control. His right lip arched upward, eyes red and aggressive. He'd been caught off guard, was contemplating recourse.

Insight darted through consciousness, eye blinks quickening, resolve firming. Jackrabbit quick, his visage shifted to ease. He had morphed, an alternate personality emerging then disappearing.

"I'm sorry. Happens when things don't go my way." He gazed gently at Eve. "I wanted everything perfect. For tonight, for you." His gaze shifted far off. "For years, I've tried to get a handle on it. My temper. But the going is slow and tough. I'm sorry."

Eve kept her distance then reached out for the gold box, tried to steady her hand.

Sam nestled the box in her hand, clearly confused. She balanced the wicked thing gracefully between fingertips and thumb. She looked at him, the box in the periphery of her vision. "Well? Where'd this come from?" Waiting for an answer, she further sensed the nature of the box's vibrations. Icy sensations pulsated but tempered, as though slowly diminishing, drawn back to an invisible realm.

Sam didn't reply. Eyes were blank. His mind seemed to scan his memory, search for an answer. Finally, he spoke, "Strange, the answer was there. I knew what to say when you asked, and now I can't remember. It's like something or someone pulled it out of my head. I never have memory problems." He squinted as he strained to recall, to no avail.

Finally, he gave up. "I just knew the box was in my pocket, and I had to give it to you."

Silence hung limply in the air. Sam stayed befuddled. An abyss grew between man and woman.

Smells of loneliness like rusted, tin garbage cans filtered through the atmosphere.

Eve didn't try to clear things up or bridge the gap. Moving forward to reach out and offer comfort was a troublesome impulse. Sam didn't know what was happening, but he did bring the box that started this crazy thing going.

Dysfunction and guys stymied about the mess they were in was an old habit. Again, things had switched. Sam was back to less than rock-solid. He stepped a tentative inch closer to Eve. Blue eyes widened, utterly dazed and mystified. Confused men were dangerous men.

Eve stepped back.

Exasperated, Sam sighed and let his arms hang limply at his side.

White-hot images seared across Eve's mind space. She saw a platinum-haired woman foul with hatred, gnarled, spewing curses. A surrealistic red tongue flicked forward and rolled across voluptuous lips. Head twisted, mien contorted, she looked insolently at Eve.

Eve forced the box back into Sam's hands. She locked his fingers over it, sealing its maleficence. "It's yours. I don't want it, won't open it."

He was shocked. "Would I hurt you?"

"Who mentioned hurting me?" Anger at high pitch, Eve needed him done and gone.

"The box brings bad. You bring bad."

Sam tossed her a final look, bruised and hard. He turned and walked the few steps to the door. Hesitated.

Eve thought, *leave*.

He slammed the door behind him.

CHAPTER 18

S am slammed his hands against the padded leather
steering wheel of his BMW. Emotions swung like a
barely-in-control carnival ride. He couldn't tell if it
was rage or love that claimed his heart. He couldn't tell which
woman he hated and which he loved. Both were seductive,
one was deadly.

Memory cleared once he left Eve's home, rage sharpening
his mind, strengthening his resolve. It wasn't hard to figure
who stood behind this foul play. Sweet Mary always needed
to be front-and-center, and anyone who interfered paid
dearly. She was the seductress, Sam the kill.

She stayed at the hacienda up till the time he left for his
date. She'd presented him with the gold box, told him not to
peek inside. Doing so was a sure way to ruin the case coming
up for trial on Monday morning. She then swept her fingers
along his brow, removing memory traces.

Sam had learned the harsh lesson to never toy with Sweet
Mary's injunctions, lest her ruthless temper unleash bad then
worse. Only once had he tempted fate. He had decided to

maneuver without her witchy blessing. Key defense witnesses grew ill, his client blabbered like a lunatic off their daily medication, and the judge copped a mood so foul that he'd sooner lock up a fragile grandma as draw the next breath.

Sam had managed a courtroom recess, calling Sweet Mary and apologizing. She cackled that infernal way that made his hairs stand on end and assured him that she'd fixed his mess. Sure enough, he went back into the courtroom, and the judge informed the court that witnesses had taken a turn for the better. Sam's client was clear-headed, sharp. The judge mysteriously morphed into a sentient being, warm and empathic as Aztlan's most respected pastor or psychotherapist.

With Sam by her side, Sweet Mary had an edge. She could influence the law. Without him, her powers couldn't weasel their way past a drunken magistrate. He brought legal bravado to the black magic pot, energy Sweet Mary extracted and deposited. Sam was the bank for one downtown bruja.

A dull headache grabbed the back of Sam's skull like a witch's claw. He hated it. He hated how he lived and what he did. He hated what he did for Sweet Mary. She had him like a rabid, feral cat dangling a sickly mouse.

Squeezing the box in the palm of his right hand, he decided to toss it—but not here, not on Eve's property. Sam slammed the car into gear, gunned the engine, and squealed the tires. The box brought bad.

Eve said it was packed with contagion. Objects could hold toxic juju. Moods changed, energy waned, things went south when bad was near. He'd seen modern voodoo in dealings with Sweet Mary, her things, knives, mirrors, stone statue used with precision to inflict psychic harm. Things inflicted hexes. He'd brought bad with him, and Sweet Mary had packed it tight. It pissed him off.

Cold nighttime air swooshed through the BMW's open windows. His mind kept clearing. The headache subsided. Rage healed a troubled lawyer's split-apart head. An image of Sweet Mary whipped across the white screen of his mind. She sat gnarled and screaming. Hideous curses rolled off her tongue. White screen of mind was like looking into a crystalline mirror.

During last evening's talk with Eve around the outdoor fire, she'd spoken of the unconscious mind. Eyes closed or open, the mind provided messages that ran along a white screen across the center of the forehead, a crystal-clear mirror.

An old bartender had once said that a man had to sacrifice to be with a good woman. He had to give up what was less to have what was more. Sweet Mary was a centuries-old witch, gnarled and gruesome with hate. She wasn't good. She was less. It was disquieting.

Sweet Mary's blood boiled. She'd finished up with the last of her well-heeled patrons. Now, nearing midnight, she closed the blinds of the little room in which she plied her trade. There was relief in the day's work being over. No taking anyone else on tonight. She was spent down past allowable reserves.

She needed to keep enough energy inside in case the unexpected popped through. Sometimes it curled up out of nowhere. Other times, it pulled out from around a corner. Sweet Mary didn't like rabbits out of hats unless she was the one who did the materializing.

Walking to her chest of drawers, she opened the top

drawer and withdrew the stained statuette. The resin warmed to her touch, a snake squirming and writhing to life. Her hands held it in check, grasped it firmly. She could squeeze it to death. She got a thrill from it.

The predator drew closer. Skin crawled, adrenaline pumped. Sweet Mary gazed into the mirror above the wooden dresser. Gaze into the mirror, gaze into the soul. He inched toward Sweet Mary in the nighttime quiet and dark. He thought no one watched. Dreams and mirrors were portals to see, to watch.

Inches from the outside door, he stood, breaths raspy against cheap wood grains that ears sensitive enough picked up—vibrations of a man, a mind-twisted man with a wrong attitude.

She waited. Her heart beat steadily. Breaths drew to capacity, rhythmic. Sweet Mary felt no concern, never did. Mastery was such an underappreciated opiate.

It was to the barrel dregs of the male species that Sweet Mary held appeal. She had raised from the dead, the mind-twisted man with a wrong attitude. He breathed lightly at her outside door. Some guys brought back to life learned quickly, others never. Sam Shear learned then forgot.

Minutes passed. There was no movement from outside the flimsy wooden door of Sweet Mary's apartment. A craving to kill emanated from Sweet Mary's pores. Hands, fingertips pulsed with ungodly desires. Sparks like static electricity shot from fingertips. Moonlight through the blinds turned morbid gray.

Sweet Mary wordlessly intoned, *Bagabi laca lama sabathani. Bagabi laca lama sabathani. Bagabi laca lama sabathani.* Primeval summoning of the wicked energy of Las Brujas Malas resonated silently. Legions of hellacious witchery quivered up from Sweet Mary's core. Her body shivered and shook. Dark gray light gyrated weird pulsations through her arms and fingers.

She relished the currents and power of a woman's might, set against a man's plotting. Men never won, but she let them think otherwise. They liked it this way. Sweet Mary salivated.

CHAPTER 19

Sam struggled, instincts pulling forward, logic yanking back harder. Temples pounding with rage, he stood at the door of Sweet Mary's apartment. It was insanity to confront Aztlan's formidable downtown bruja.

Impulses to break into Sweet Mary's apartment swept through mind and body. The strain of holding back was fracturing his mind. Nerves were way past edgy and frayed. Sweet Mary had been there for him when everyone else had bailed, but the price was everything.

She had been mother, diviner, voodoo woman extraordinaire. Sam's own mother specialized in use and abuse. She'd left him in a psychic heap. Mother never should have had a kid. Hers was devotion to cocaine then the old religion of Aztlan. She left one addiction, turned to another. One bad habit morphed into another, more sinister obsession. Religious creed swallowed her whole.

Sweet Mary found down-and-out Sam splattered against the grimy alley wall. He'd been ready to turn out the lights for good. Sweet Mary swooped in, and there'd be no living, breathing Sam Shear without Sweet Mary.

Kicking in the door would end it. Beads of sweat rolled down Sam's temples. There'd be no making up or apologies. Once Sweet Mary had been crossed, there'd be no hiding from the downtown witch's fury. He didn't dare knock. That'd be as foolish as a mouse asking entrance into a black cat's domain. Sweet Mary sensed things from afar. He had to move quickly, no turning back.

Stepping a couple of paces from the door, he got ready to kick in the flimsy pine panels. An image of Eve shot across his mental screen. He stopped. Listening to street-smart instinct kept the downtown lawyer alive. His mind was keener than ever to mental flashes, emotional stirrings, subtle energy shifts. Warnings stirred.

An autumn midnight atmosphere grew rank with smells of embittered souls. It curled the stomach like sour milk. It overwhelmed the senses like backed-up sewage. Sam wiped his hand across his nose.

A rank smell came from the crumbling edifice next to her apartment. He now knew it was the Palace of the Queen of Death, Michté. From mildewed walls, Michté screamed the incantation of witches long gone yet ever present. *Bagabi laca lama sabathani. Bagabi laca lama sabathani. Bagabi laca lama sabathani.* The horrid chant echoed in his mind.

Heart clenched, chest pain nearly forced him to knees. Things spun, and the night atmosphere squeezed down. He wanted to drop. He made himself stay strong, upright.

Words rang on. *Bagabi laca lama sabathani. Bagabi laca lama sabathani. Bagabi laca lama sabathani.* Intonation shifted, soothing, seductive as a bevy of enchantresses.

An urge to gently turn the doorknob gripped tight. He knew it was open. Sweet Mary was waiting with open arms.

He snapped to. He stepped back. He pressed against the back guardrail. He'd nearly lost balance.

An image of Eve surfaced like a cool breeze on a muggy night. It was a steadying force. His mind cleared, body regained balance, resolve strengthened. He had to deal with Sweet Mary. She was an oppression. She *was* oppression. She was Mother who would not let go.

He slammed his right foot into the flimsy, weather-beaten door. It cracked in two. Everything was a blur. Seconds and milliseconds whipped by. He stepped past the threshold into the dimly lit room. It stank of cigarettes and beer. Smells of coitus wafted through the atmosphere like decades-old cockroaches buried in mildewed walls. Silence draped itself like black mold through the dingy quarters.

He was alone.

Torn and faded green wallpaper and red velvet, moth-eaten curtains bordered the decay-ridden room of Aztlan's reigning bruja. It stank of gut rot from wild parties and foggy memories. It was swimming underwater in a fetid pond.

Sam turned to look at the door. It was intact. Distinctly, he recalled the crash and splintering of flimsy pine boards. His right leg and foot ached. Yet the door stood in one rickety piece, wood grain curling wraith-like, pointing, glaring.

He was alone.

Eerie sensations, ghosts whispering, electrical currents prickling skin pressed in from every direction of the dank quarters. Hairs stood on end along the back of his neck and on his arms. He was being watched.

One second, eyes popped out from under the bed then from behind stained curtains, only to dart around a corner brass floor lamp. Bed covers spontaneously rippled across a sunken mattress, then were thrown off, and jumbled into a heap that resembled a corpse in the fetal position. Sheets were twisted, stained. Sweet Mary worked with gusto. Her black magic tore through the room like electric currents sparking and smoking from loose wiring.

His eyes shot to the bathroom. It was closed. Visions of Sweet Mother Mary waiting chock-full of nastiness flew through a lawyer's flustered mind. He thought about blasting into the tiny chamber of purgation. It'd be like sticking his hand down a rattler's hole.

Sweet Mary had a plethora of jack-in-the-box antics up her witch's sleeve. Background checked by private investigators, Sam discovered she was of the secret clan of Las Brujas Malas. She'd never told him, wasn't the confiding sort.

The Clan of Las Brujas was known only through hearsay since not a soul had ever seen the women, save one spoken of in hushed voices as Michté, whom Sam now recognized as Sweet Mary, Queen of Death.

After initial inquiries, private investigators refused to look into the matter further since their business had taken a quick downturn the instant they commenced the investigation. Easiest to most difficult cases deteriorated. Not an investigation could be solved, simply finding a way out of a proverbial brown paper bag of a routine case proving a formidable challenge.

Clients left investigators' offices upset and demanding full refunds. One private eye after another complained some kind of a god-awful spell had been cast, stopping professional instincts from working properly. A gray shroud hemmed them in on all sides, couldn't do investigative work any more than a two-by-four could cut through steel.

Out of desperation, the last of the PIs had visited an old seer and healer in a metaphysical bookstore. She had a reputation among locals of spotting when evil was at work. In her tiny candlelit room, she assisted earnest souls. Sitting across from him at her desk, she closed her eyes as he laid the tops of his hands down on her desk as instructed.

Three or four seconds after touching his hands lightly, she pulled away and calmly stated, "Miché has cursed you. If you do not stop the investigation, she will destroy your business and bring your life to ruination."

The seer did not say which of his professional investigations had generated the curse. But to the badly shaken private investigator, it was obvious as lightning across a desert mesa on an otherwise placid night. By month's end, after resigning from the job, business picked up for the greatly relieved fellow. To this day, three years later, he refused all work from Sam.

The rusted bathroom doorknob turned. It squeaked then twisted with a horrid grating. Chills curled up Sam's spine. The thing kept turning, spun round and round, out of control, and squeaking freakishly.

Malodorous gusts intensified in the room. Sam covered his nostrils with the palm of his hand and quashed his nausea. Windows were shut tight, front door closed. A pounding blast and the bathroom door flew open.

Sam flew back a couple of steps, heart beating erratically. Blood pressure rang in his eardrums. He wobbled, footing unsure, wouldn't have been surprised if the floor buckled and caved. Wrong was happening and passing as quick as bats flying out of Carlsbad Caverns on a stone-cold and spooky desert night. Underworld howls ripped out of the bathroom.

Sam's eyes opened wide and high as waves of sewage stink further overwhelmed a sturdy man. He cupped both hands over nose and mouth and pressed hard as the bridge of his nose could endure. Ear-splitting shrieks like denizens of crazed coyotes kicked into a nerve-rattling and deafening loudness that drove him to his knees.

An explosion beneath the commode ripped and blew out the back wall. Porcelain chunks flew in every direction. He covered his head with forearms and elbows. Sharp pieces gashed at the back of his hands and exposed neckline.

Then things quieted. They came to a hush. Sam looked out from between tightly laced fingers. Smoke trailed out of the dingy bathroom. They curled into index fingers, swarming through the room, and then morphed into gnarly female hands and fingers. They scratched at Sam's head, neck, and throat, squeezing tight and viciously.

He spat and found his rage and inched toward the bathroom, moving into swirling smoke and demolished back wall. Smoke cleared. The room breathed of nighttime air gone from wretched to fresh. The remaining sidewall held a medicine cabinet, mirror above inscribed with red lipstick, *Sweet Mary + Sam the Man — Mother + Son… Forever.*

Sam smashed at the tarnished mirror with the padding of his fists. It didn't break. Sweet Mary had said it was cut from the same glass as the old one in the barroom next door. It was cursed. Sweet Mary used the old mirrors, the one in the bar, and the one in the bathroom. She maneuvered through it and, legend held, would one day witness how it turned the tide of life, fate, and destiny.

Sam ripped it off the wall and left with it securely in hand.

CHAPTER 20

Sweet Mary entered the shadowy, underground, limestone cavern. Spirits screamed from the mirror shards embedded in the walls. Pointed and gnarled female fingers were inscribed into scarred and stained limestone block. They pointed downward.

Sweet Mary stepped down the stone steps. Lethal underworld gases contaminated the atmosphere. It was air she loved to breathe, stings along the lining of her lungs an exquisite pleasure. Mists dense as storm clouds swirled nervously.

Dead rodents and cockroaches littered the shadowy pathway. Lives of embittered souls reeked like carcass stink, butchered cows and bulls, haunting the winding stairwell. Flickering specters in mirror shards of castrated bulls, testicles served sizzling hot on an iron pan, graced the ghostly ambience.

Sweet Mary removed the bricks that held the leather-bound copy of *The Malleus Maleficarum*, the ancient text of 1484 used by Las Brujas to conjure special curses. She opened it and read,

> *Tormented by the devil without intermission…*
> *he was deprived of the sane use of words,*
> *yet he was always conscious of his words,*
> *though not of their meaning…*

Michté stirred within Sweet Mary. She sensed the dark inspiration as a thrill that heated head to toe. It sizzled the core of her being with anticipation. Teachings from the old book brought forth a visceral rousing of primal witchery. She felt wet. Desirous. Death was the ultimate discharge, release.

Michté had awoken, Sweet Mary no more. Michté gazed into the largest shard of smoky mirror fixed to a section of blackened limestone. She needed to fix her intent, psychic energy. She would concentrate at the third eye. It would burn. The mirror would scream.

Fiery emotion mixed with black magic would crack the mirror. It groaned with unearthly sounds, of troubled men and dying dogs. They were a cacophony of hideous screams from centuries of men who'd lost their way, and women who'd lost theirs trying to help them. The old mirror absorbed Michté's white-hot hate. It was an old and foul magic. It relied on hate. It sent hate. Hate got what it wanted and tossed scraps to the side.

Michté screamed, "*Bagabi laca lama sabathani! Bagabi laca lama sabathani! Bagabi laca lama sabathani!*" Over and over, the incantation resounded, the chant reverberating at high pitch. Witchy powers intensified from white-hot to a nearly invisible dark luminescence.

The mirror cracked.

Wailings of the damned shook the building, dust

streaming from the ceiling. A choir of tortured beings roared the ungodly refrain, *"Bagabi laca lama sabathani! Bagabi laca lama sabathani! Bagabi laca lama sabathani!"*

A rusted steel door leading to the deepest basement, center point of Abyss of the Witches, appeared along one wall. Michté touched it and it opened. Malevolent energy exhaled smells of urine and fresh feces. The sealed portal had been unlocked.

Never had it been entered since a century past. Those who'd tried and touched the door had vanished. The marks of their fingertips could be seen up and down the steel encasement. Ashes were smeared into the foundation. They were of witches who'd attempted entrance and failed. Their hate had been shallow. Sweet Mary's hate was not shallow. She screamed. She blazed with hatred, face hot, body drenched with sweat.

A spiral, iron staircase wound its way thirty feet into the damp earth. Bone-chilling cold grabbed hold of Michté. She preferred it to Aztlan's sun-drenched days.

Bagabi laca lama sabathani. Bagabi laca lama sabathani. Bagabi laca lama sabathani.

Queen of Death, intoxicated by the vibratory powers of the inner chant, stepped down and into the lowest abode of violent emotion, thwarted lives, and unending stories of lost love.

Bagabi laca lama sabathani. Bagabi laca lama sabathani. Bagabi laca lama sabathani.

Men craved what childhood failed to provide. Sweet Mary became Mother, Sweet Mother, Sweet Mary Mother, Michté.

Bagabi laca lama sabathani. Bagabi laca lama sabathani. Bagabi laca lama sabathani.

Sweet Mary took the last turn along the iron spiral staircase. Touching her foot to the ground, netherworld lights flickered on. Dark luminescence glowed from beneath cracks and crevices of a stone foundation. Bass vibrations and a high-pitched cacophony of shrieking from invisible sources rose in unison to welcome the Queen of Death.

Quivering forms slithered out from the basement's shadowy alcoves. Darkness assumed human shape. Las Brujas Malas materialized. Infernal spirits of Geralda, Orlinda, and Hortensia glided to the foot of the stairs where Michté waited.

Conjuring demanded collectively garnered demonic energy. Descending into the Abyss of the Witches concentrated the baleful energies of the coven. Las Brujas Malas made men pay.

And tonight, they would make one man pay, mercilessly. Man wanted out of mother's keeping. This had not been the agreement. He must pay.

"*Brujas!*" Michté shrieked. Dust shook loose from wooden ceiling rafters. "*Brujas mias!*" she wailed with hellish vigor of women scorned by men whose love had wandered.

"*Bagabi laca lama sabathani! Bagabi laca lama sabathani! Bagabi laca lama sabathani!*"

Wailing in unison, they sang the song of unrequited love. "*Bagabi laca lama sabathani! Bagabi laca lama sabathani! Bagabi laca lama sabathani!*" Witches, at the command of the Queen of Death, set forth their might and unleashed a terrible energy. Screeching reverberated through brick and mortar, dirt and dust. "*Bagabi laca lama sabathani! Bagabi laca lama sabathani! Bagabi laca lama sabathani!*"

Michté furthered her concentration on the words of ancient text:

Tormented by the devil without intermission…
he was deprived of the sane use of words,
yet he was always conscious of his words,
though not of their meaning…

Sam Shear needed his words.

"*Bagabi laca lama sabathani!* *Bagabi laca lama sabathani!* *Bagabi laca lama sabathani!*"

CHAPTER 21

E ve slept fitfully. While dreaming, she felt herself twisting her sheets into knots. They wrapped around her torso like undulating snakes. Quetzalcoatl, uniter of heaven and earth, swept through the nightscape of her dreams. Feathered serpent, god of light, mercy, and wind, ruled the mythic skies of Aztlan. Lord of morning star, death, and resurrection, he reigned without peer among ancient gods. He presided as a deity of blood, sacrifice, and underworld dominion.

Throughout the night, she'd been troubled by dark and violent images. She was a little girl of the pueblo, counseling an abandoned mother who wanted to die and made a little girl feel responsible to keep her alive. She was deep in the forest with the medicine women of Aztlan as scholar and researcher, learning of ritual practices to ward off evil. She was a learned woman fending off men of crazed minds and wayward libidos.

All night had been a struggle against good and bad. Love and no love, bad love and good love were a jumbled mess.

Love flickered and faded like an electrical conduit plugged in then unplugged.

She made the ascent from the world of sleeping and dreams to wakefulness. The journey was fraught with uncertainty. She feared becoming stuck in the other realm. Those who desired to die, consciously or unconsciously, did not abide for long in the world of the living. They died at surprising times. She wondered about complicity in matters of untimely death.

Slowly, she opened her eyes. She felt hesitant. The night's tossing often portended the challenges of the day. A fitful night, a fitful day. Eve prepared herself mentally. She remained in bed and closed her eyes, gathered her energy. The day could not be anticipated.

She concentrated energy at her brow point. The area between her eyes warmed. After a few moments, she looked out the far sheer-covered window. From her bed, she saw the overcast day. A dingy gray lighting appeared as a contaminant in the normally sun-drenched realm of Aztlan.

Dark and unsettling, the light shimmered as though a threatening presence lurked beneath daylight. Intuition stirred, urging Eve to see Graciéla. But she was dead. Yet, how could she be dead? The woman of wisdom and natural magic could not be dead. How could one so wise suffer death when so much was left undone?

Eve knew Graciéla *was* dead. She sighed as grief opened wide. Eve's mind traveled between memories and reality. She'd become disoriented by the intensity of sleep and dreaming. For a moment, she wasn't sure if she were awake or asleep. She rubbed her eyes and tried to reorient.

Graciéla seemed palpably close. She thought she smelled the scent of her freshly washed cotton clothes, fabric dried in the Aztlan sun. She thought she sensed the presence of Graciéla, warmth flushing through her core. Eve needed to feel Graciéla, be near Graciéla, talk with Graciéla. She needed to visit the bookstore, the place where natural magic had been conjured.

The gloominess of the day reflected the night's torment, shadowy forces of sorcery and deceit warned of in dream after dream. Quetzalcoatl presided over otherworldly practices, shedding of blood close at hand. Graciéla had always sensed sinister happenings from afar, would advise as a shamanic helper to one forewarned by the Lord of Life and Destruction.

Even in death, Graciéla came as helper and guide. To those of mystic sense, death heightened what was present in life. Mystically, Graciéla was alive, closer in death than in life, and Eve was grateful.

Reenergized, she got out of bed quickly and went to shower. As she turned on the water, it nearly scalded her. She pulled back. "Damn. What the fuck?" It was never this hot so quickly. She tempered the heat and stepped under the water's cascading rhythm.

Steam curled up from the shower drain. Smells of sulphur rose. She felt the urge to vomit.

The front doorbell rang. No one visited at seven in the morning. Canvassers flocked the neighborhood before and after work. She waited. The foul odor passed, as did the nausea.

The doorbell didn't ring again. They'd come back if it was important. The day was off to a strange start.

Temperate water continued to flow. Eve didn't trust the temperature, so didn't lather for long. Getting in and out of the shower quickly seemed safest.

Scents of last night's incense and candle, lit before going to bed, wafted through the air as she stepped out of the morning rinse. She needed to finish and get to the bookstore.

Graciéla's spirit beckoned.

Parking along the side street adjoining the metaphysical shop, Eve stepped out of her car.

She tapped the hood, a little insurance against getting broken into in downtown Aztlan del Sur. Eyes constantly peered out from unsuspected places and thieves got in and out quicker than mice through crevices in decrepit buildings.

She cast a quick glance down the street. A sudden concern came over her for Gabriél, her trusted cab driver and mysterious protector. She'd get to the bookstore, and then try to get in touch with him. He usually appeared out of nowhere when she needed a ride or simply to talk.

Suddenly, her breath caught. The outer world faded in, then out. She felt faint, steadied herself against her car. A vision of Gabriél lit up along the white space of her mind. It was vague, flickered, but she could see his outreached hand and look of pain cross his face.

He was as an angel, smitten by a nefarious hand. Surrounding him were a gathering of kindred spirits, benevolent and powerful. Their presence glowed with a blinding luminescence in the midst of a battle both psychic and of this world.

The vision passed. She caught her breath, but heart rate slowed only slightly. Worry continued, an image lingering in the background of her mind.

A cab drove by on one of the side streets. It sped up once past the speed bump, obviously hurried to get deeper into downtown. The car was there one second and gone the next, rapidly escaping from Eve's sight.

She couldn't make out the driver. But the car was like Gabriél's two-decades-old sedan. He seemed to be on duty morning, noon, and night.

The angst dropped and settled like a brick somewhere inside Eve's gut. She struggled to let it go, not obsess, as she was prone to do when matters of friendship and love were at stake. The cab was headed toward the oldest area of downtown, the location of the crumbling limestone church.

She'd have to tend to her worries for her friend later. First, she needed to visit the bookstore. There, she would find guidance to see her through escalating troubles.

At a brisk pace, Eve walked the half block to the bookstore. Gazing upward, she enjoyed the sight of the now cloudless, blue sky, a constant source of consolation. The dim radiance of early morning had dispersed. The air breathed pure and dry, intoxication of the mile-high atmosphere lifting her spirits.

The brass bells above the bookshop door sounded their familiar ring. Eve stepped inside. Red candles glowed warmly. Piñon incense curled through the atmosphere. Books on chakras, yoga, meditation, philosophy, and other esoteric subjects lined the walls. In the middle of the store stood wooden cases of stones, candles, audiotapes, and flutes.

Behind the back counter, absorbedly reading a book, sat Rachel. She was the absentee store owner who lived reclusively up north in her home along the banks of the Chama River. Graciéla had agreed to be the store manager rather than Rachel closing the veritable bookstore upon her retirement. Rachel had returned to Aztlan del Sur as soon as possible after having learned of Graciéla's death.

She looked up and nodded. "I've been waiting for you."

Eve hadn't called. Rachel was an intuitive sort. Rachel and Graciéla had been close. Eve knew they were kindred souls, and Rachel had suffered from Graciéla's passing. She had not attended Graciéla's memorial, preferring to mourn privately.

Once, when Eve had applied for tenure and underwent stress-induced night sweats, Rachel called her one evening. She said that she needn't worry. All would be well. Eve hadn't confided in either Graciéla or Rachel. The next day, the department chair informed Eve that she had been granted full professorship and tenure. Synchronous events and uncanny coincidences surrounded Graciéla and Rachel.

"I've needed to stop by." Eve approached the now reigning seventy-three-year-old spiritual matriarch of downtown Aztlan del Sur. In Rachel's presence, as with Graciéla's, Eve felt a sense of calm.

Rachel smiled warmly. She stood no more than five-foot-two, skin leathery brown, burnished from years of farming along the Chama River before coming into town to open the bookstore. She had always wanted to engage with spiritual seekers. A metaphysical store allowed for spiritual exchange and friendship. She came out from behind the counter, arms outstretched, her tightly packed and sturdy frame offering warmth and caring.

Eve felt a sudden urge to cry. "I've been missing Graciéla. I just needed to be here. To linger where we used to meet and talk."

Rachel held her close then, after a few moments, took a

step back and looked into Eve's teary eyes with a soft yet soul-penetrating gaze. "Talk with me, Eve," she said, barely above a whisper.

Eve knew the words were for herself, not for Rachel. She, like Graciéla, understood immediately, wordlessly. Words were for those who needed to speak and find relief from disorder and hiddenness. Quietness was for those who already knew.

Eve didn't answer right away. She felt lost, disoriented, and not sure why she stood befuddled before the sage. It was as though Graciéla had sent her.

Rachel smiled gently. She slowly moved behind the counter then toward the back of the store. "Come to the kitchen, Eve. We need to talk in private. Just as you and Graciéla did."

She walked into the kitchen. "I do not take Graciéla's place. No one can do that. But I am here as a friend." She paused, looked toward the place where Graciéla passed on, eyes tearing, and then moved toward the cupboards. "I'll make some green tea for us. Just got a fresh delivery from the Mountain Road Tea Company. It's delicious."

Eve sat at the tiny pine breakfast table, a familiar and settling place. Graciéla sat across from her. The feeling left Eve stunned. Eve laid her hands on the table and looked at the empty chair. Peacefulness wafted through the kitchen like piñon incense.

The water boiled quickly, Rachel lifting the strainer from the well-used green and red earthenware pot. Green tea lifted the spirits midmorning and helped rouse dormant energy midafternoon. Tea was a matter of soul.

Rachel brought the cups of tea to the table and stirred in a teaspoon of Aztlan honey, a daily medicinal thought to ward off allergies. "May our conversation breathe forth wisdom for us today, Eve." She nodded, raised her cup, and together, they took the first sip of the fragrant brew.

"Delicious." Eve's taste buds streamed with pleasant, aromatic sensations. She always had looked forward to tea and talk with Graciéla, ritual relaxing into reverie and a flow of words and emotion.

Words came hard for Eve. A well-educated woman, a professor, proficient in logic and research, was often befuddled by human emotion. Graciéla's sensitive touch with silence, words, and feeling were instructive and healing.

Rachel sensed her musing. "You miss her. I miss her too. Take your tea." They sipped in silence. "It's a blend of green tea and lavender from Aztlan del Norte, medicine for a troubled soul."

Eve smiled. "Well, I could use a special kind of soul medicine today." After a few moments, Eve felt the urge to speak. She wanted to detail her dealings with Sam as she would have with Graciéla. She wanted to talk about the little evil box and her vision, ask what she should do.

Rachel, sensing Eve's pressing needs, drew a deep breath. "As we sat, I smelled scents of nature, wildflowers, cedar, and heard the sound of winds blowing through mountain canyons. *Gah'e*, protective mountain spirits, encircled you, empowering you." A hush swept through the small room, chills moving up Eve's spine, whiffs of piñon trees and cedar fires in the kiva wafting through the air.

Rachel closed her eyes. She leaned farther back in her chair. "Gah'e grows more intense, Eve." She gently touched the tip of her right index finger to her brow point. Scents of fields of mountain wildflowers drifted through the kitchen.

The front door bells chimed.

Rachel stayed seated. "You answer the door, Eve."

A brief hesitation then Eve left the kitchen. She entered back into the store, looked around the softly lit, numinous setting. In her mind's eye, there appeared protective presences, faint movements of light.

Graciéla stood near the door. Her presence was strong. She met Eve's eyes with resolve and fearlessness.

The middle of Eve's forehead became hot.

The door opened of its own accord and Eve left.

CHAPTER 22

The day passed uneventfully for Eve. She was both relieved and put off by it. She'd wanted things to happen, anything. She needed to act and put her concerns to rest. But it had to be at the right time.

Timing is everything, Eve.

After running errands, she'd gone by the university to tend to a few unfinished tasks, and then went for a run along the foothills. She wanted to feel near Sam.

By day's end, she was spent. Rachel's guidance had been perfect, yet she felt so alone. There was really no one to turn to any longer, no one to listen whenever she needed to talk. Rachel was a good friend, but the feeling between them was different than with Graciéla. She was on her own.

That night, she nestled into her bed. Descent into the dream world was rocky. She entered a light sleep of fitful dreaming, not unknown to an anxious soul. Then she dropped deeper into sleep, wrapped in a twilight realm of desert light and far-off voices.

She saw fields of dream-sized wildflowers. They bore the

same scent as those in the bookstore earlier that day. Breezes started up in the dream. They turned to winds, substantial and loud. The winds swirled in patterns, reminding Eve of a Hoffman symphony she had recently listened to. They were rhythmic, majestic, surprising. Air currents coalesced into spirits.

Eve reclined on a low-lying stonewall. They were like the ones constructed by Aztlan masons as borders between farmhouses and tracts of land. Stonework undulated as gargantuan snakes twisting their way across hills and valleys. Darkness thickened and spirits flew by.

Eve was now twenty feet above ground, still on the stonewall. She looked down. Dizziness descended as though from within and without at once. She felt the wall sway. Humpty-Dumpty had a great fall. You couldn't put Humpty-Dumpty together again. It was the tune sung by her mother as she tried to soothe Eve to sleep. It didn't work. As a child, she'd sat on a wall then jumped down and played in the grass beneath a great cottonwood tree. She pictured this as she lay in bed as a child, and then drifted into a sleep often tormented and frequently nightmarish.

Here she could not jump down. Humpty-Dumpty had a great fall. Had a great fall. Had a great fall. All the king's horses and all the king's men couldn't put Humpty together again. Again. Again.

She clung to the wall. She couldn't move. Thoughts of her mother and falling apart crowded into her head. She wanted to squeeze her temples. But she couldn't move. Her mother had fallen apart and the neural pathway was carved in Eve's brain and psyche to crack and crinkle as her mother had, into millions of shattered mind pieces.

Thoughts of a little girl taking care of her mother crowded

into her head. She wanted to squeeze her temples. But she couldn't move. She couldn't take care of her mother. She couldn't take care of herself. A grown woman needed to take care of herself, not crack and crinkle into millions of shattered mind pieces.

She was a child. Alone. She had to take care of a mother who had fallen apart and couldn't be put back together again. Her mind teetered, snap, snap, snapping close to breaking. And Humpty Dumpty had a great fall.

Vibrations rose from within the earth. The ground swelled and then dropped into great crevices that ripped across the darkened countryside. She saw into the earth, its core molten.

Red currents of lava and fire gurgled beneath the surface. The earth cried to erupt but could not. It swelled and dropped and swelled once more.

Eve gripped the edges of the stonewall, clung white-knuckle tight. She could fall. She could be swallowed by one of the many crevices opening around her. There were cracks in the earth, in the mind, in the woman who sat on the wall and feared a great fall.

Dizziness struck. But she had to get off. She had to get off the in-between place. She had to get off.

"NOW! NOW! NOW!" A commanding voice ripped the dreamworld. The sound shot up through the center of the steaming and red-hot terrain.

Eve flung herself off the wall. She ran and ran. Across the erupting earth, she ran. She did not lose her breath. Strength rippled through her lungs and muscles. She could go on and never look back.

She ran down the country slope of the pitch-black dreamscape then suddenly stopped. The earth cracked wide, at least fifty yards long and wide, in front of her. The twilight scene crackled with the energy of phantasms rippling through air currents. They were angels and devils bustling expectantly.

The voice spoke again, more without than within this time. "She comes."

From out of the crevice arose a dark form. Atmospheric currents undulated furiously. They shifted into otherworldly forms, women of ages past, present, and to come. They gathered round the dark feminine spirit that emerged from within the deepest places of the earth.

There surged an intonation from women past, present, and to come.

> *She is lone and she is wild*
> *She is Goddess of the Wild Thing*
> *Her shout is as loud as thunder*
> *Her breath as mighty winds*
> *Her eyes flames of fire*
> *She is moving*
> *She is coming*
> *She is near*

Thrill and panic lit through Eve. Her sensitivities burned white hot. Before her rose a sixty-foot supernatural being. Waves and particles of sparkling darkness wavered then coalesced, and the dark divinity ascended to the sky.

Goddess.

Tonatzé.

Eve fell to her knees. Supernatural energies coursed through her. She wept.

Bagabi laca lama sabathani. Bagabi laca lama sabathani.

The words pounded in Sam's head during sleep. He struggled against the infernal sounds, sheets damp and twisted. Hatred laced a winding and knotted path through the infernal syllables, each word a snake hissing and writhing. He tensed and turned in his bed, wrestling against evil.

The sheets were wet with sweat, pillow like a sponge. The words echoed. *Bagabi laca lama sabathani. Bagabi laca lama sabathani.* He'd hoped to get three or four hours of sleep. But there'd be no rest. He was tormented by Sweet Mary, her voice, her curse.

She used the malicious words during rituals. They were hatred, targeted and sure. He'd seen their terrible effects. And now, it was at him they were aimed. Sweet Mary worked foul magic from afar.

His thoughts were riveted on the downtown witch even as he tried to pry himself awake. Finally, he jettisoned out of the dreamworld by a sheer act of will. He bolted out of bed. Time was at a premium.

He readied himself and left the hacienda in less than ten minutes, swerved onto the freeway and drove well past the speed limit from the foothills of the Aztlan del Sur Mountains to his downtown office. Minutes flew by like bats out of a Carlsbad cave.

There'd been no finding Sweet Mary last night. Dives, tree-covered parks, and alleyways turned up empty. She dwelt in shadows and was impossible to discover—unless she willed it.

Sam pressed the button to roll down the windows of his BMW. The mile-high air was crisp and fresh. It breathed like an exquisite mix of oxygen and high-desert scents of sage, autumn grasses, and cedar from burning in pueblo *ornos.*

Adrenaline shot through his system, hypercharging a man set on finishing a task too long postponed.

Usually, he got out of the house before six a.m., but this morning seven o'clock had to do since he'd been out till three a.m.

A bizarre thing suddenly happened. His tongue spontaneously coiled, became dry and coarse. It was being twisted off and clumped. It curled tight like a lump of old and dry dog shit left on a downtown street in the heat of midday summer.

Sweet Mary's raging face blasted through his mind. Sam cursed her, in his mind let loose a stream of street words foul and rage-filled. He despised her and did not hold the feeling back.

His tongue snapped loose like the lash of a whip. His neck snapped back. His jaws clenched tighter than normal. His every muscle tightened beyond what felt like a breaking point. Palms squeezed tightly against the black leather steering wheel; he thought he could have bent or busted it.

He flashed on Sweet Mary's neck. A twist and a snap, and that would be that for Sweet Mary Quite Contrary. She wanted what she wanted, and she wanted Sam. There was no compromise for Sweet Mary, and there'd be no compromise for Sam. There was no love between them, never had been love. Sweet Mary did not do love. Sam saw it and saw it clear as noonday sun on a wide-open mesa. He could live with that. Rage swelled. It was not a loss of temper. It was temper targeted and set.

CHAPTER 23

Michté screamed yet again. Packs of rats scurried into decades-old holes in walls and floors. They clawed and chewed into red brick, making crevices larger, more sharply ragged.

"*Bagabi laca lama sabathani. Bagabi laca lama sabathani. Bagabi laca lama sabathani,*" she howled as she stood in the midst of the desecrated palace of hate. The loud curse crumbled mortar and turned brick to dust. Gray clouds clogged the atmosphere. Eeriness thickened and settled into the basement cavern.

The dust that had clung to walls soaked up underground moisture and dripped thick as paste onto the moist dirt floor. The walls bled Sweet Mary's hatred for no good men. They wanted freedom from the mother. It was not meant to be. Sweet Mary willed it not to be. Sam defied her; Sweet Mary willed him not to be.

Geralda, Orlinda, and Hortensia morphed into one thin stream of smoke. They entered through a large hole in the center of the packed-earth basement. Theirs was a violence hidden within the bowels of corrupted Mother Earth, within the rancid breast of Michté, Queen of Death. Michté breathed deeply of the deadly gases. The vapors rose from hidden reservoirs beneath this abandoned limestone church. It escaped from cracks, crevices, and stonewalls.

The vile exhaust of a weary mother twisted and curled beneath compacted soil. It pressed against the periphery of the building's innermost foundation. It pushed against the edges of a teetering and condemned building. The building cracked and groaned, buttresses and joints bulging. It was the center point of the unfathomable void that was Las Brujas Malas.

Hatred screamed out of the four brujas. It breathed forth from their phantasmagoric lungs. They, four-made-one, were the Queen of Death. Decades of men had succumbed to her lures. Memories flitted to mind as moths before a raging bonfire. They had been unaware of the evil within a woman scorned and mother love turned bad.

Decay fed on decay. Witchy women fed on lifeless men. Each needed the other. No wallowing man escaped the grasp of Michté. The abrogado was good as gone. He thought he found true love. Sweet Mary would show him true love gone bad.

Fury grew to an even higher pitch. The Queen of Death howled as fiercely as northerly winds across wide-open stretches of exposed desert mesa. Arm muscles bulging, veins rippled coarsely across her forearms and biceps. She was Queen of Death, Michté. And never had she felt so strong. Her heart was stone. Love was not woman's to have. Michté, Queen of Death, knew love was not woman's to have. Woman's lot was hatred made of stone.

Shifts of psychic currents slammed into the vast

underground chamber. Limestone blocks plummeted and crashed to the ground, sprays of grit and dust dense with soot shot through the atmosphere. Earth shook hard as a midsummer quake through distant mountains. Walls crumbled inward, layer after thin layer of tiny spiders, flicked from their complex webs, rained down into blackness.

Michté held her head erect amid falling debris and contemplated her powers. She smiled. It was wickedness borne from generations of women with hearts of stone. Feverishly, she rocked on her feet. Violent vibrations rumbled atop and beneath wet, packed earth. Tremors cracked through the underworld domain and made the entire brick edifice waver.

Michté's eyes widened, she sniffed the air. There was opposing energy, scents of wildflowers and centuries of womanhood innocent and searching. Goddess of woman unsullied, wildness unscathed, placed at risk were well-crafted strategies and tragic endings conjured by the Queen of Death.

Tonatzé, the Goddess of the Wild Thing, of love and birth, ancient enemy of all things maleficent, watched from a world of veiled powers and behind-the-scenes natural magic.

Michté howled. Tonatzé's influence was subtle. She could catch a predatory witch by her sharpened talons and dash her to the ground were she not vigilant—hypervigilant. Michté scanned the scene for invisible presences not of her ilk. There was energy, daring and strong, but not yet here. Michté knew of this force but had never before encountered her, one subtle and yet clear as moonlight streaming on a cloudless night.

She was the Goddess of the Wild Thing, one whose shout was loud as thunder, breath as mighty winds, eyes the flames of fire. She was near. She was near.

Michté shuddered. She fought against the weakness. Hatred ripped out of her belly and she howled. Weakness vanished. Walls ceased undulating. The spot between the brow points burned red hot.

The ancient Goddess of Love could have come closer. She toyed with Michté. This should not be done. Tonatzé should not have dared toy with Michté, Queen of Death. Tonatzé was older magic. She wound through corridors of time as sweet burning sage through carved passageways of Anasazi ruins. The old places depicted the calling, summoning of The Goddess, words inscribed in granite:

Vocatus atque non vocoatus, Deus aderit.
Vocatus atque non vocoatus, Deus aderit.
Vocatus atque non vocoatus, Deus aderit.

Summoned or not, the Goddess comes. The Goddess had been summoned. Michté knew of the old summoning. But summoned or not, the wild Goddess could appear. She came when need grew strong. Michté despised strength. It alone prohibited her black magic. Strength was rare.

She cursed and spat and spat again. Legions of spiders flew from their crevices into the air and disintegrated. They sacrificed themselves as testament to spirits of women and mothers and daughters sacrificed to Michté. Michté closed her eyes, bent forward, and shrieked.

Before the twist and turn of psychic events with Tonatzé, Michté would exact her lot. The earth shook, walls crumbled inward, and layer after miniscule layer of tiny spiders jettisoned from their complex webs and rained into the blackness of the mouth of Michté.

Quietly, the four women gathered in the spacious back yoga and meditation room of the metaphysical bookshop. Once again, it was the time for their shared Saturday morning vinyasa yoga practice. The ancient discipline nourished strength and focus.

A side window was left ajar to permit the filtering through of crisp morning air. Scents of fallen yellow cottonwood, elm leaves, and damp morning earth in nearby gardens graced the interior yogic practice space. Welcome scents, they hearkened to psychic depths.

Anticipation sparked the atmosphere. Into a semicircle, they formed a hallowed drawing together. Silence enveloped the room and blanketed each woman as a warm covering for chilled flesh.

Graciéla had for years hosted their Saturday morning spiritual ritual that mobilized and focused psychic energies. Rachel wanted them to continue the spiritual custom. It was a summoning of powers that conjured good and exorcised bad.

Clean, light, one-hundred-year-old oaken planks, waxed and perfectly aligned, afforded earthy grounding for women devoted to yogic energies of earth, air, fire, water, and ether, symbols of the Goddess of the Wild Thing, Tonatzé.

Eve placed her red mat in front of a sixteenth-century Asian teak altar Rachel had discovered at a local backyard sale and brought to the store specifically for the yoginis. It was three feet wide and a foot deep, ample room for candles, flowers, and incense. A picture of Kali, East Indian representation of the one the four yoginis knew as Tonatzé, presided over the ancient ritual.

Yoginis of old considered Kali the black one, Goddess of time and change. She held all things in order, obliterated obstacles, and annihilated the bad that interfered with the coming of the good. Her presence graced the room with intense feminine energy, fiery and blood red.

Shirley, red hair uncombed and wild as Aztlan brush fires, positioned her black mat next to Eve's. Samantha and Tanya rolled their red mats across the dimly lit bamboo floor on either side of Shirley and Eve. No one spoke.

Candles burned steadily, and smoke from Nag Champa incense graced the fresh air pleasantly and sweetly. Sitting in lotus posture for a few minutes with eyes closed, they centered themselves. A profound quieting of the soul was evident as inhalations and exhalations flowed rhythmically. For years, the tranquil yet intense energy graced their natural expression of yogic breath and movement.

Each reported that a week's missed practice triggered bewildering challenges, minds ill at ease and bodies fractious. A month's missing would have borne bouts of excessive eating, drinking, and foul moods. Disruption of psychic discipline interrupted natural patterns, synchronistic energy, and left a strong woman weak.

They were not weak, happenings of late fortifying their resolve to not permit disruption in their practice, focus, and strength.

Silently, the four rose to their feet as if drawn upward by an invisible reality. They stood at the top of their mats and initiated the familiar sequencing of yoga postures. Coordinated and audible deep nostril breathing aligned movement with respiration.

Gliding along, bodies agile and supple, they engaged in

the sacred sequencing of yoga poses.

Beads of perspiration formed across brows and exposed skin, glistening droplets of perspiration dotting yoga mats. They continued quietly, a forceful concentration of mind and body. Sages held that yogic practice summoned spirits. The space spiritually charged, mind and soul quickening to what had been missed, to what lay ahead.

One hour passed. Each yogini was transported mentally and physically into bliss. Yoga released stress, calmed the nervous system, healing hormones revitalizing organs, muscles, sinews, and tendons. Energy lit through body and mind.

Without warning, thunder boomed, shook the window-panes, and reverberated through walls and across floorboards, jolting the four out of their yogic trance.

"Wow," Shirley remarked, her shoulder-length red hair flicking across her shoulders like lightning across mountain skies. The other three didn't speak.

Another boom rattled the windowpanes like a bag of old bones. The tallest red glass candle holder teetered atop the table then cracked and shattered like a rifle shot at close range.

Shards of red glass weirdly coalesced in midair and flew at the yoginis, propelled by an unseen and vicious presence. Flurries of red danced about the room as sprays of red light gyrated in a menacing dance. Creepily, they molded into a straight line and sped, arrow sharp, at their stunned and doe-eyed target.

Eve cried out, hands cupped over eyes, her shrill voice betraying terrible pain and shock. Blood oozed between splayed fingers pressed white across her cheeks. She curled fetally and moaned. A cry arose from within her, a sounding of thousands of wailing women, voices echoing through sandstone canyons of time.

Shirley cradled Eve, gently so as to not worsen injury or discomfort. Stunned, Shirley looked at Samantha and Tanya. They circled round Eve. Shirley pressed gently to examine the injury, a doctor's sensitive touch. Inspecting jaws and cheeks, there was nothing of consequence. She bent forward and tenderly moved Eve's fingers away from her eyes. "Let me see. I'll take care of you."

Worry lines creased Shirley's forehead as she examined the inflamed and bloodied wound. Tears formed. Sweat dripped from her brow. "Laceration, but nothing appears embedded. Stay still. Don't tilt back in case there's something I don't see. Could have embedded itself far below the surface. Turn on the lights. I need to get a closer look."

Harsh atmospheric charges and weird changes of light swept through the room, a gray hue hanging low and pressing down, sucking the air out of the atmosphere. Shirley gasped, as did the Samantha and Tanya. They steadied themselves, caught their breath, moved on to tend to Eve.

Shirley's hair hovered inches above her shoulders as her eyes fixated worriedly on her friend. Samantha stood up and turned on the overhead light. She hurried out of the room to the back kitchen where Rachel kept a first-aid box.

The yoga room was dim, presences from a shadowy realm having intruded, a sinister energy wafting through the small area like inescapable, toxic fumes.

Samantha came back to the yoga room and knelt beside her friend. She opened the first-aid kit and removed a sealed alcohol swab and an extra-large Band-Aid. Examining the sight again, her brows furrowed, her gaze intense. "There *was* nothing embedded. Far as I could see, there was nothing there. But *now*... looks like... not sure, but we need to get to the emergency room… STAT." Worry lines creased forehead to lips. "Let's go. One of you drive, I'll sit in the back with Eve."

Evil drew closer. She stroked Eve's forehead and whispered, "Be strong, we are here. We'll see you through."

"I'll drive." Tanya stood up and walked quickly toward the bench where their shoes and purses were. She looked at Samantha, who stayed next to Shirley and Eve as though she hadn't heard Shirley's firm voice. "Samantha. Let's go. Come on."

"I'm just not sure we should move her. There's something bad here, more than medicine can fix. It's foul magic. We need to focus our energies. That'll exorcise the evil." Samantha's eyes were wide and glassy.

Shirley bypassed her. "Help me here, Tanya. We'll both get her to the car. We don't have time for energetic healing. We need surgery."

Eve moaned. She rolled her head slowly from side to side. Her eyes rolled to the back of her head. Sweeping her hands over her eyes, she strained to focus on her three friends.

They gasped.

Eyes rolled back again. Breathing ceased. Head tilted sideways.

CHAPTER 24

E ve drifted to a high-desert place, a realm of clouds and mists where memories of earth faded. She was in an etheric land. The atmosphere was turquoise bright. Its sky was cloudless and the air crisp and clean. Lucid dreaming was a familiar state. She knew how to be aware of dreaming while dreaming. Yet, this was other than that. She had made the Great Passage.

She hovered outside of time and space, a realm of pure spirit. Graciéla appeared, spirit beside spirit. They embraced, tears flowing. Graciéla sat on the stone outcropping next to Eve.

Wordlessly she communicated. *There are universes beyond our ken. This is one. It is within, and it is beyond. It exists in the mists. They are the memories of Goddess.*

Eve was not at rest. Things were strange. She did not want to be here. She could not deny the comfort of it, of being with Graciéla. But she was not at rest. This was not right. She did not want to be in this arid place of sweet consolation.

In the background of her mind, she heard her friends,

worried and frightened. She heard their anxious words. *Evil is here. It struck and will strike again. Eve can't leave us.*

Graciéla too had heard and responded. *Nothing more to be done. Nothing more to be said. Be still.*

Moments passed in silence before Graciéla interrupted the quiet and Eve's grieving. *The yoga stopped the worst from happening, but it was not strong enough.* Graciéla looked away and into the distance, her eyes roaming the ethereal expanse of desert from atop the hallowed plateau.

Everything grew even more still. Mists formed out of desert stone crevices and caressed distant mountain peaks. It was a world of haunted beauty.

Eve did not belong here. She did not want to be here. Her friends, their worried voices, echoed on in her mind. She looked at Graciéla. Her old friend did not seem the same. She was different, resigned. There were no wrinkles, no spots from the sun, so much gone from the Graciéla she'd known and loved.

Eve's life had ceased, friends abandoned, love, hoped for and worked hard for, gone. Love was to be no more. Eve raised her head to the sky and gritted her teeth. There were no tears in her, for the days of tears were over. The time for hope was over. In this place of bliss, there was no hope for there was nothing to hope for, no striving, no strain, and no pain. Eve did not want to be here. She did not want this heaven.

Graciéla looked to the ground, a woman alone with granite and sandstone chips, pebbles, stones, and boulders fashioned in orderly patterns on the smooth-surfaced earth. This was eternal equanimity. Evil had come and exacted its due.

Sadness welled again; rage welled and quickened. It set

loose a force. It went out of from Eve like north winds through mountain canyons. Gray clouds formed, thunder clapped, and rains began and turned to streams then to floods rushing through arroyos, carving their way down a treacherous mountainside.

Floods overtook the land, and vast terrains of low-lying shrub and distant pine trees shriveled and withered, the territory morphing into a hazy gray and lifeless plateau. Dense, dark clouds descended farther from mountain heights and mists and canopied the stony setting like a wool blanket, soaked and heavy. Sadness pressed violently upon the landscape like the smudging of a once-beating heart against flattened stone.

Eve watched, waited, and felt deeply in her body, her muscles and sinews tingling. Rage grew to an even higher pitch, muscles straining. Rage was a wind, gale terrifying, winding its way through Sandia Mountain heights. Crossing over had been quick. Eve had entered the land of the passing, the world of souls making their way. It wasn't as she imagined.

She watched as stones and earth cascaded downward. She shook her head and struggled to break free of this realm where streaks of wind, gray and swirling, now brushed through the atmosphere. Their sweep was wide and harsh.

Graciéla stroked her head, moving the palm of her hand from Eve's head to her neck, warmth emanating from the sage and seer. *There is nothing more to be done. Nothing more to be said. Be still.*

Eve jerked away. She would not be still. She felt she could not trust her old friend. Graciéla told her to yield. This was not like Graciéla. In life or in death, this was not like Graciéla.

Eve knew of the age-old practice of soul-making. Teacher,

trickster, and sage, Graciéla was always up to something. Graciéla winked.

Gray gave way to jabs of black, and rains became violent. Violence cracked through the dark skies as lightning and thunder illuminated the darkness. The surreal great, stony desert of mystic Aztlan swelled, lands undulating as a pregnant Goddess in labor.

The Goddess arose from beneath the wet and loamy earth of the realm of passing and eternal equanimity and ascended past the parting gray mists and dense clouds. Her shout was loud as thunder, breath as mighty winds, eyes as flames of fire.

CHAPTER 25

Samantha, Tanya, and Shirley had agreed to gather at Eve's home, in her backyard on a full moon autumn night, three days after Eve's accident. It was an unseasonably chilly, misty, and full moon time. Yellowing cottonwood leaves hung precipitously from decades-old branches. Some clung to lone branches edging their way toward inevitable descent.

The night's atmosphere breathed an unearthliness that chilled the most intrepid of souls. The three women nestled under the cover of the oldest and largest cottonwoods near the grotto of the Goddess. Grass grew under the great tree despite its shade, Eve saying that some grasses required coolness and shade just as some vegetables were most nourished by the light of the moon.

Shock had come and gone. Over the course of the past three days, the friends had mourned and wept. Life's most startling of events had shaken them to their core. The prospect of death held an unanticipated shock.

In her own inimitable way, Graciéla had taken hold of

matters. Psyches invigorated by yoga, Samantha, Tanya, and Shirley had dreamed of her. She had come to them from a far-off place resembling Aztlan in the most dreamlike of ways.

"I saw a world of astonishing beauty and multiple dimensions, vivid and startlingly real." The others nodded in agreement with Samantha's description of her dream.

Tanya added, "Piñon trees were sixty feet tall, boughs surrealistically plentiful with nuts. Skies were a radiant turquoise blue."

Shirley closed her eyes in remembrance and continued, "Crisp high-mountain air whirled in patterns wild and free, pure white clouds supple and shifting with winds that caressed the skin like an exotic balm."

They each sighed, comforted by the sharing. Intuitively, they'd known of their common experience since each saw the others in their nighttime dreamscape.

In a series of three dreams, Graciéla told each of the friends to go to Eve's backyard that night. Rachel called on the third day and said a note had been left for them at the metaphysical store. She had discovered it that morning in a desk drawer she hadn't opened since Graciéla's passing. It was marked for the three friends, Rachel instructed to hold it unopened.

They went to the store earlier in the evening. Shirley opened the letter in the presence of her two friends and Rachel. In Graciéla's handwriting, Shirley read, "A practitioner of black magic known as Michté has levied an assault against Eve. Yogic practitioners through the ages have taught that the psychic realm opens during asana practice. Both good and bad energies hover at the ready to enter open chakras."

Shirley, fingers trembling and breathing rapidly, stopped midway through the letter. The others remained quiet. She swallowed and drew a deep breath. "Psychic centers absorb healing or can be injured depending on the disposition of the mind. You four were in a weakened state because of grief, Eve the weakest because of her travails."

Shirley paused, looked at her friends, eyes tearing as she read, "Despair is the most terrible of mental toxins." Graciéla's letter, written as if she were standing in the back kitchen over a cup of tea, emphasized that in spite of the weakness, yoga had cut the evil short. "I have no time to explain further. Events will reveal the truth. Soon, all will learn of the unknown foe and the dangers of living too close to the edge."

Shirley finished reading, and the four women left for Eve's home as Graciéla instructed. Rachel was to accompany them for she alone was old enough to know what was about to take place. She knew the world of mystic Aztlan and its mysteries. Rachel was there as a witness.

In the nighttime-still backyard, the four gathered in a circle and breathed deeply, naturally, rhythmically. Chills ran up their forearms and necks. Each shuddered as light currents of electricity rippled through the air and across their bodies.

Breathing became a yogic mantra, *ajapa*, soundless mantra. The sound of breath alone was heard from throat to deep exhalation. Heads swayed, bodies lulled into meditative absorption as the four remained seated in lotus posture on the grass near the grotto of the Goddess.

Yoga propagated mantras to invoke the protection of the Goddess, but Eve eschewed religious doctrines. She'd taken to heart Graciéla's teaching and the instruction of the medicine women of Aztlan. "The force of the human personality conjures healing energies, mantra simply an assist." She taught a simple mantra, ajapa, mantra of breath.

She used it to concentrate powers of the mind. It conjured the powers of Tonatzé especially in times of conflict and severe danger.

Breaths grew slower, deeper, and more full-throated, air through the larynx like nighttime whispers through mountain aspen. Tonight, six large beeswax candles were lit in the grotto of the Goddess. The four friends, sitting cross-legged in a circle before the hallowed altar, saw the tiny flames from their mystic third eye point. Eyes closed, they concentrated on the flames.

The heat intensified brow point to solar plexus. They opened their eyes. The mirror behind the stone sculpture became vaporous. It was a portal to an unseen dimension. The flames, casting their warm glow, projected shadows of guardian spirits shimmering across the small back lawn. Lingering scents of sage burned minutes earlier heightened their psychic senses. They had entered a realm familiar yet, tonight, uniquely strange.

Years ago, they had agreed to enter this hallowed spirit realm should one of their number make passage to the high place of the stony desert. It was a sacred realm of clouds and mists where memories of earth faded. From within its depths, the Goddess was said to arise.

Joining hands, they locked tight psychic energies, breaths nearly inaudible. Then, they gently constricted their throats as they breathed, releasing inhalations and exhalations, primal breezes in the night. They deepened their meditative state.

As Eve many times said, "Meditation prepares for entrance into the spirit world. Senses calmed, illuminating energies come forth. Agitation attracts bad spirits. Ajapa soothes the mind and draws benevolent energies."

They wanted what was best for Eve, and they had no way of knowing what that was despite their grief, misgivings, and wondering.

There was a shift in the atmosphere. Their breaths were imperceptible. The air grew warmer. Inner vision was opened. The mystic third eye revealed an interior nocturnal landscape, stars emanating an otherworldly luminosity, a gargantuan moon, blue and full, hovering watchfully, expectantly.

A desert great horned owl was perched in a large pine tree. It sounded, *hoo… hoo… hoo… hoo*. The high pitch of the female howl rose and lingered in the surreal realm of deep mind and old specters.

Among shamanic cultures, owls pierced illusions. They provided sight into the darkness of the mind. Able to outfly the golden eagle, its talons like the paws of a small mountain lion, as carnivorous as a small beast, the great horned owl of the mystic realm was a surreal and prodigious force of truth.

In the night, they spotted their prey from up to two thousand feet away. They retained supernatural hearing. Bearers of the mysteries of shamanism and witchcraft, they served as guides through dark tunnels into worlds unknown and foreboding.

Tanya, Shirley, Samantha, and Rachel gazed upward at the gargantuan great horned desert owl. The owl flew away from the tree then turned and hovered above the sacred coven, directing them to follow where she led.

They traveled through layers of time and space, currents of energy quivering as they made passage between mystic demesnes. Eternities passed as they traversed through psychic planes of desert and high mountains and lands, moonlike and numinous. After what seemed like years, they arrived at a chthonic realm within the earth where Michté, Queen of the Death, presided over the bones of the dead.

CHAPTER 26

Michté loomed large like a nefarious deity rising out of a dank and putrid earth. She hovered in the epicenter of a realm barely visible to the mystically trained eye. Wicked darkness did not permit traces of ordinary light. Michté was raw, malevolent energy. She leaned her head backward and roared with a fury so forceful that hyperextended blood vessels ready to burst ripped across her forehead.

She shifted into a wicked and black great horned owl and attacked, left the underground chamber, flew past the crumbling limestone structure above her dank cavern, and swooped down into Eve's hallowed backyard.

The transition happened in milliseconds. The four friends followed, shape-shifted and transformed into gray great horned owls with large heads and enormous wings, charging upward toward the raptor visage of Michté. Feathers flew in six directions, north, south, east, west, above, and below, in accord with sacred Aztlan tradition. Feathers swirled in circular patterns. Howling winds obscured the airborne battle now in the darkened backyard.

There was a great crash that startled and alarmed the evil horned owl even as she fought against the four smaller owls. Another bigger owl, with eyes brown and fierce as the noonday sun, had jettisoned into position from an unknown dimension. It attacked the evil horned owl and propelled her back through space and time—a portal but not before swipes of claws and impaling of beak shredded her skin and tore away feathers.

The great horned owls, now five strong, followed the evil raptor through the mystic portal and flew above the crumbling limestone edifice that was her abode and whose walls were graffitied with black soot. The walls read: Bagabi laca lama sabathani. Bagabi laca lama sabathani. Bagabi laca lama sabathani.

The five great horned owls knew the limestone walls stood as a befouled guardian around the dank underground chambers of the evil witch, Michté. If they hesitated in making this final stand, death would be quick, and theirs would be an ultimate descent into the unhallowed realm of liars, fools, and desperate souls.

They gazed at the moldering orifices in the walls, an ecclesiastical structure leaning inward on the brink of collapse, intermittent holes in great blocks of limestone appearing to suck in and never expel. Darkness eroded oxygen. Walls and rank atmosphere extinguished human breath and left nothing but air so stale that human lungs threatened to collapse. The great horned owls breathed from within themselves as yoginis masterful with breath control.

In spirit, the five hovered in flight in the deepest recesses of Michté's lair as legions of rats clawed at the discolored walls, their grating ear-piercing. The walls leaned farther inward and teetered as a ravenous maw. The five owls remained side by side in the cavern beneath the street level of downtown Aztlan del Sur, where the abandoned and desecrated limestone church stood.

The shadowy surroundings offered minimal sight. Miché, presence reeking as a rotting corpse, hovered menacingly. Stumbling, feeble, and disoriented, her visage shifted to a maleficent witch. Her shadow spanned over thirty feet of the crumbling limestone walls.

Flames encircled and radiated from the Queen of Death. Engulfed in flames, Miché emanated searing energy. Coldness, not heat, radiated from the flames. Tips of fire encrusted with a blue iciness set frigidity into muscles, tendons, and bones of the five owls.

The Queen of Death flung her head ever farther backward, gazing upwards toward the heavens. Legions of women howled from her gaping orifice. *"Bagabi laca lama sabathani. Bagabi laca lama sabathani. Bagabi laca lama sabathani."*

Swirling legions of spirits and seraphs flew at Miché. She pointed a gnarled right index finger at the most powerful of heavenly hosts. She again cried out the curse, and the seraph's light dimmed, appeared to falter and descend into an abyss. Companion spirits scattered as luminescence waned against the age-old intonation.

The five great horned owls prepared to swoop down and attack. A great crash came, and glass rained down from the dark and towering rooftop. The Queen of Death was taken by surprise, her blue eyes widening.

The seraphs reappeared, the most powerful at the center. Energy and light intensified; they surrounded Miché. She morphed into an old, twisted, and knotted Queen. She tried to screech forth the foul words but no sound came.

The apparition of the Queen of Death wavered then dissipated. A flickering of white, blue, and faint reds oscillated through the cavern's shadowy atmosphere. It seemed smaller, less imposing. Ice-blue waves undulated through the desolate and dark confinement of a woman's terrible lies and despair.

The five great horned owls had ceased their flight and hovered safely to the side under a limestone cove. They watched as the showering glass twisted and turned through the darkened realm. Jettisoning shards of the old mirror did not injure them, invisibly repelled.

Reflections of Eve, Samantha, Shirley, and Tanya at Los Muertos Cantina shimmered through the dank underworld as triangulated mirror bits drifted and floated in the sulphuric atmosphere. Images of men, promises spoken, promises broken, despair secreted away shattered as reflections in the mirror splintered into bits and became crystalline dust.

The specter of Michté faded and flickered. Violently, she gasped through her horribly widened nostrils, cold blue eyes sickeningly misshapen like chunks of twisted clay. Her corneas, red and engorged, popped and splintered, crystallized and turned to dust.

Psychic traces of Michté tried to howl and shriek. Again, no sound came from her twisted mouth. The gargantuan shadow of the Queen of Death, Michté, flickered a few more times, then dissipated as a wisp of a dust devil's last dance.

Stunned, Shirley, Tanya, Samantha, and Rachel awoke, having shifted from one world to the next, one form to another. They were back in Eve's yard at nighttime, encircled about the grotto of the Goddess, the statue no longer present on the altar in front of the antique mirror.

Bits of mirror lay crumbled about the stone grotto. The earth felt warm to the touch, the night no longer chilly. Powerful and good, the great horned owl of the visionary realm was perched atop the backyard's aged cottonwood tree, green eyes quiet and observing.

Mists surrounded the four friends, and from the back entrance to the yard, beyond the wooden gate, there appeared two figures. Through vapors and mist, they emerged as spirits moving from one realm to the next.

Shirley looked; the great horned desert owl was no longer perched atop the cottonwood. Graciéla walked forward, Eve beside her, into the hallowed circle of women. Their faces were illuminated by an unearthly radiance. The Nag Champa incense of the yoga practice room emanated from Eve and Graciéla. Eve's countenance was otherworldly, light radiating from her brown eyes. Hesitation, doubt, loneliness were gone.

Samantha, Shirley, Tanya, and Rachel, psychic senses charged from heightened consciousness, intuited the making of a soul.

Graciéla, urban shaman knowledgeable in ancient ways of soul-making, had entered the realm of the great stone desert. There she bore witness as the Goddess wept the tears of no love and bore witness to the great sadness, now as a distorted reflection in an old mirror. Mists of a time gone by and memories of Goddesses past and to come, she who was lone and she who is wild, she who is the Goddess of the Wild Thing, shout as loud as thunder, breath as mighty winds, eyes flames of fire.

Two hours earlier, Eve had been released from the Intensive

Care Unit of Downtown Aztlan Hospital, neurologists having discharged the first patient they had ever successfully treated for acute hypnic cortical trauma. Patients entered a profound coma from which recovery was rare if at all. Research noted that those who did recover, reported dreamlike apparitions and life-changing encounters in a world of phantasms where they were given another chance, another day to set things right. Discharge happened within hours of awakening since vital signs returned to normal, and often the patients were more robust than ever before in their medical history.

Eve vividly remembered Graciéla, as mentor, guide, envoy of the Goddess of things wild and free, of love and loneliness borne and abandoned, making passage with her from the realm of the high stony desert.

They emerged from the backyard mists, Graciéla staying at a remove as Eve drew closer to be with friends, shaken but resolved.

Sam stood in the street outside Eve's home, a man relieved and intent on his future with the woman for whom he had risked everything. Beneath him, on the midnight-darkened street, lay relics of the obliterated mirror of Los Muertos Cantina. A dump truck loaded with remnants of the cursed mirror and demolished limestone edifice offered proof of his actions. A full moon hung low, reflecting the light of the eternal feminine deity from the scattered bits of glass on the street as mists curled about the asphalt expanse.

Six ethereal figures, one at a remove, walked out of Eve's backyard. They looked at the strewn debris. Things had been brought to a fateful end. Eve had called Sam to pick her up from the hospital. He was the one who needed to be there. He was the one she wanted to see, to be with, to love now and for the future, for all that it would bring.

Less than an hour earlier, Sam had completed what he needed to do. A furious man intent on seeing to the end what had long been put off, he had not been able to discover the whereabouts of his foe. But through the lens of ages past, the woman of love lost and never found was revealed.

He purchased the old looking glass of Los Muertos Cantina, its reflections in the full-moon night, glimmering images of a downtown abandoned limestone edifice, beneath which resided the abyss of the woman of love lost and never found, Michté, Queen of Death.

After calling in favors from municipal bureaucrats, he took the mirror to the old limestone church. He had it hoisted by crane and propitiously dropped, then slammed it with wrecking balls, time and again on the ancient edifice of love lost and never found.

Sam stood still as the women looked on the pile of debris, the broken mirror, and limestone rubble speaking to them of a deed completed, destruction thwarted, and life yet to be lived. He stood strong, hands to his side, earnest and intent.

At the corner of the street, under the old wooden light pole, a cab was parked. There was a quick flicker of its headlight. Gabriél got out, closed the door, and rested against the car, a kind smile creasing his face.

And Shirley, Tanya, Samantha, and Rachel spontaneously intoned, "She who is wild, Goddess of the Wild Thing, shout as loud as thunder, breath as mighty winds, eyes flames of fire. She is here. She is here." Twice more they sang the verse.

Eve was quiet, still dazed from the impact of the moment. Then she felt the words echo on from within her, *She who is wild, Goddess of the Wild Thing, shout as loud as thunder, breath as mighty winds, eyes flames of fire. She is here. She is here.* Twice more the words soundlessly echoed. She closed her eyes then opened them and turned to Graciéla.

The spirit of Graciéla leaned toward her. *Time has come to make your way. To move on. And for me to move on. This is the time of my true passing—and yours. Mists of the sadness of no love and memories gone by are fleeting as distorted reflections in an old and warbled mirror.* She disappeared into the night.

Eve drew near to Sam. They watched the full moon, the ancient deity of love, brighten and hover protectively over the gothic city of Aztlan del Sur.

CONNECT WITH PAUL DEBLASSIE III:

www.pauldeblassieiii.com

Twitter: @pdeblassieiii
Facebook: @pdeblassieiii